THE HUSBAND HUNTERS

Andrina had made up her mind.

Her two lovely sisters—orphaned, penniless, buried in the country—would never find suitable husbands. Andrina would go to London and impose on her godfather, the Duke of Broxbourne, to introduce the girls to society. Her sisters' beauty would accomplish the rest.

As she watched her younger sisters sparkle at the endless round of balls and receptions, Andrina marveled at how well her plan had been realized.

There was only one snag: Andrina had been so busy arranging her sisters' futures, she failed to notice she was madly in love.

BARBARA CARTLAND

Barbara Cartland

THE
HUSBAND HUNTERS

BANTAM BOOKS
TORONTO · NEW YORK · LONDON

THE HUSBAND HUNTERS
A Bantam Book / May 1976

Published simultaneously in the United States and Canada

Bantam Books are published by Bantam Books, Inc. Its trade-
mark, consisting of the words "Bantam Books" and the por-
trayal of a bantam, is registered in the United States Patent
Office and in other countries. Marca Registrada. Bantam
Books, Inc., 666 Fifth Avenue, New York, New York 10019.

PRINTED IN THE UNITED STATES OF AMERICA

CHAPTER ONE

1816

"I have solved the problem!"

The door of the Breakfast-Room had burst open as the gay, lilting voice continued:

"I lay awake all night thinking about it, and now I know exactly what we must do!"

Her entrance caused the two young women sitting at the table to turn their faces towards her and there was instant eagerness in two pairs of eyes as they replied:

"What have you decided? Tell us, Andrina, quickly!"

Andrina walked into the room to sit down at the head of the table.

It would have been difficult looking at the three sisters to imagine that there could be anywhere in the world three girls who were each so exquisitely beautiful, but each so different.

Andrina was the oldest and least spectacular.

Her second sister, Cheryl, was at eighteen and a half so lovely that most people on seeing her were struck speechless by her appearance.

She had golden hair, the colour of ripening corn, blue eyes—the translucent blue of a thrush's egg—and a pink-and-white complexion which reminded people irresistibly of strawberries and cream.

What was more, she had a slim, elegant figure and moved gracefully.

Sharon, her younger sister, took after her father and was dark-haired with a magnolia-like skin and eyes that

1

were sometimes blue and sometimes purple in their depths.

Colonel Maldon had always said that Sharon was a throw-back to a Spanish ancestor who had occurred somewhere in the Maldon family-tree; but whatever ancestor she resembled, Sharon was lovely and also the wittiest and the gayest of the three sisters.

She found everything amusing and was insatiably curious about life and people. She longed for the social whirl which she read about in the ladies' magazines and occasionally in the more sedate *Morning Post*, which her father had taken every day.

Andrina would have been outstanding in any company which did not include her sisters, but if she appeared to compromise between them it was because her hair was neither fair nor dark.

"Mousy" she herself called it disparagingly, but her mother had always said firmly that it was the "colour of a shadow which people found comforting and protective after the glare of the sunshine."

As if to complement her hair, Andrina's eyes were grey, although in some lights they appeared to be green, and she thought despondently that nature might have been kind enough to give her red hair to go with them. Her face, however, had a sweeter expression than her two sisters' faces had.

Because she was the oldest she had forced herself to be the practical one and after her mother's death five years ago she had, even though she had been little over fifteen at the time, taken complete control of the household.

Her father had been ill during the last two years of his life and, Cheryl and Sharon being so young, it was left to Andrina to be hostess, housekeeper, nurse, teacher, and maid-of-all-work.

The girls had a Governess who came in from the village.

But it was Andrina who had remembered and passed on all her mother had taught her, and it was she who had instilled into Cheryl and Sharon the exquisite good manners which Mrs. Maldon had thought essential, the rules of etiquette which every young lady should follow, and all the other qualities which Andrina thought her mother would expect to find in each of her daughters.

They had been quite easy to manage, not only because they loved Andrina but also because Cheryl was far too good-natured not to agree to anything that was suggested to her, while Sharon was exceedingly ambitious.

It was Sharon who had put the idea into Andrina's head which she had puzzled over during the night, and which now seemed to burst from her lips as she said:

"I have decided that I must go to London immediately!"

"To London?" Sharon exclaimed. "But what for? And why you?"

"I will tell you," Andrina answered, helping herself to coffee from a pot that stood in front of her on the table before she continued:

"I lay awake thinking of what you said to me last night, Sharon."

"What I said," Sharon interposed, "was that if the two Miss Gunnings could take London by storm, we could do the same. And what is more, there are three of us!"

"You also said," Cheryl remarked, "that you thought I was lovelier than Elizabeth Gunning and that Andrina looked rather like Maria."

"Yes, that is what I said," Sharon agreed. "But I—"

"And that is exactly what I have been thinking about," Andrina interrupted. "It is perfectly true—you are both lovely, far more lovely than I am—but I should have come with you to look after you."

She paused for a moment, then added:

"Let us face facts. We are not going to be able to live here in any comfort, much less in any luxury, on what Papa has left."

"What is it exactly?" Sharon asked.

Andrina drew in her breath.

"Under two hundred pounds a year!" she said. "We

own the house, but it is badly in need of repair, and I do not see, if we are to feed and clothe ourselves, that we can afford more than one horse on that income."

There was silence as both her sisters looked at her apprehensively, before Andrina went on:

"That is why, when I was feeling desperate, a solution came to me."

"What is it?" Sharon asked. "Tell us quickly!"

"I am going to London to see the Duke!"

"The Duke?" her sister echoed. "What Duke? I had no idea we knew one!"

"We have never met him," Andrina replied, "but Papa said he was a very distant relative, and he is my godfather."

"Not a very good one," Sharon said scornfully. "As far as I know he has never sent you a present!"

"He has never paid the slightest attention to me," Andrina replied, "and that is why it is about time he did!"

"Who is he?" Cheryl asked.

"The Duke of Broxbourne," Andrina replied. "He must be getting very old, but Papa was fond of him. When he was young he used to go with his father to stay with the Duke, and he once described to me how grand and important the house was."

"Why did he become your godfather?" Cheryl enquired.

Andrina smiled.

"I am not certain, but I am sure it was due to Mama. You know how she always wanted us to know what she called 'nice people,' and she and Papa moved in Society before he lost everything through gambling."

"How could he have been so stupid?" Sharon asked angrily.

"That is what he often used to ask himself," Andrina said. "He was always bitterly ashamed of having thrown away his inheritance in such a stupid manner! But I dare say it was difficult when all the gentlemen whom Papa knew were gambling wildly in London

Clubs and he, being so gay and handsome, would have been unable to resist following their lead."

"I can understand that while he was still unmarried," Sharon said, "but you would have thought Mama would have been able to restrain him."

"She tried," Andrina replied, "but she said herself she was so young and thoughtless, and, as you know, she adored Papa and always wanted him to be happy."

"It is not very happy for us now," Sharon said.

"Yes, I know," Andrina agreed, "and that is why I intend to see the Duke and insist that he do something."

"How can you insist?" Cheryl enquired.

"I am not certain," Andrina answered. "Perhaps his conscience will prick him when he realises that he has neglected not only Papa as a friend and relative but also all of us down the years since we came to live here."

"Papa once said," Sharon remarked, "that the rich have no use for the paupers sitting outside their front gates."

"That is obviously what the Duke thinks," Andrina said, "and I am going to point out to His Grace that the very least he can do is to introduce us to Society and help you both to find yourselves husbands."

"Husbands?" Cheryl ejaculated.

"Of course," Andrina answered. "Why else should you go to London?"

"Yes, you are quite right," Sharon exclaimed. "That is what the Gunning sisters did. Elizabeth married a Duke—two Dukes for that matter—and Marie an Earl!"

The story had always been one of Andrina's favourites.

The two desperately poor sisters had come with their mother from Ireland in 1751 to take London Society by storm. Newspapers chronicled their movements; verses in their praise filled the magazines:

> *Bright Aetherials! Matchless Pair;*
> *Modest, Lovely, Blooming, Fair.*

Having known Elizabeth only a month, the Duke of Hamilton offered her his hand and heart, and they were married at midnight in the Great Chapel in Curzon Street.

Five days later Maria married the Earl of Coventry and set out for Lord Ashburnham's seat at Charlton in Kent "to consummate their nuptials."

Not only beautiful, Elizabeth was loyal, sympathetic, brave, and compassionate—qualities which were very necessary when she found that she had married a notorious drunkard.

However, after two children had been born, one being a son and heir, the Duke, worn out by intemperance, died at age thirty-three.

Elizabeth, lonely and unhappy, soon married again. Her second husband was Colonel Ian Campbell, a man of high character and noble ambitions, who later became the Fifth Duke of Argyll.

To Andrina it was the most romantic story she knew, and as she thought about it she was sure that Elizabeth Gunning could have been no more beautiful than Cheryl.

"You too must marry a Duke," Cheryl was saying to Sharon. "I personally think it would be frightening to be a Duchess!"

"I would love to see you a Duchess, Cheryl," Andrina interposed. "There can never have been a more beautiful one, and I know that when we reach London every man who sees you will propose to you—except those who are proposing to Sharon!"

"What about you?" Cheryl asked.

"I shall have no time to think about myself until you are both safely settled," Andrina replied, "and you know, girls, that it is a question of urgency. We shall have just enough money for this Season only—one Season and no more!"

"How shall we have even that?" Sharon asked.

"Have you forgotten Mama's necklace?" Andrina asked softly.

Both her sisters gave an exclamation at the same time.

"Mama's necklace—of course!" Sharon cried. "It must be worth hundreds of pounds!"

"Except for the emeralds, the stones are not very big," Andrina replied. "But Mama told me once that she was certain, if she sold it, she could get five hundred pounds for it!"

"That is a lot of money!" Cheryl exclaimed.

"It will be enough for our purpose," Andrina said. "Do not forget, the reason Mama kept it hidden all the years we have lived here was that it should be a little 'nest-egg' for us, should we ever need it."

"I wonder why Papa did not make her sell it," Sharon said.

"She persuaded him first to put it on one side, and later I think he forgot about it," Andrina answered. "Anyway, I know she would have sold it if any of us had married, and now we are going to sell it for that very reason."

"If we get five hundred pounds for it," Sharon said practically, "that would be almost a hundred sixty-seven pounds each!"

"Yes, if we divided the money equally between us," Andrina agreed. "But as a lump sum it will be enough for us to rent a house in London for the next two months and to buy some pretty new gowns."

"The Gunnings had only one between them!" Sharon remarked.

"You are going to have more than that," Andrina said. "I have a feeling that people have grown more sophisticated than when the Gunning girls first caused such a sensation."

"The gowns are simpler," Sharon replied, "but there is less of them—very much less! *The Ladies' Magazine* said last week—'Fashions from Paris adopted by the girls at Vauxhall and other places are the thinnest muslins offering glimpses of breasts and legs to ardent young men.' "

"Sharon!" Andrina exclaimed. "I have never heard

anything so improper! You and Cheryl will wear nothing of the sort!"

"We have to be in the fashion, Andrina!" Sharon retorted. *"La Belle Assemblée* said that 'Ladies in a most reprehensible manner in Paris and in London are damping their muslins so as to make them cling to their figures so that they appear almost naked'!"

"I cannot think what sort of *ladies* they are talking about!" Andrina said sharply. "You will be modest if nothing else! I am quite certain the type of husband I want for you would not wish his wife to look fast or improper!"

"We will do whatever you want us to do," Cheryl said.

Andrina smiled at her and her eyes softened.

"Thank you, Cheryl. I want you to trust me and believe I know what is best for you both. It is terribly important that we should not do anything wrong or appear in London under the wrong auspices."

"That is true," Sharon agreed, "and the most important thing, far more important than anything else, is for us to get into Almack's!"

"What is Almack's?" Cheryl asked.

Both sisters looked at Sharon, who, although she was only just over seventeen, always had more knowledge of the fashionable world than either of them.

"Almack's," she replied, "is the most exclusive and the most important supper-and-dancing Club in the whole of London."

"Tell us about it," Cheryl begged.

"I have read all about it," Sharon answered, "and it is ruled by a group of patronesses such as Lady Jersey, Lady Castlereagh, Lady Cowper, the Princess de Lieven, and several others."

She paused to look at her two sisters and say dramatically:

"If one does not get on the List and receive a voucher-invitation issued by one of the Patronesses, then you cannot visit Almack's and you are a complete social outcast!"

"It sounds very snobby!" Andrina remarked.

"That is what they want it to be," Sharon answered.

She rose from the table.

"I will read you a poem. I found it in one of the magazines last year. I know where it is."

She ran from the room and Andrina looked at Cheryl.

She looked exquisitely beautiful in the spring sunshine coming through the window which had just touched her hair and turned it into living gold.

Andrina bent forward, a smile on her lips, to say:

"You cannot stay here, Cheryl, dearest, meeting no-one and seeing no-one but Hugo Renton."

"But I like Hugo," Cheryl protested.

"He is a very nice young man," Andrina agreed, "but you know as well as I do that he has no money of his own, and his father would put every obstacle in the way of your marrying him. Besides, Hugo is of little importance except here in Cheshire, and there are all sorts of exciting young men waiting for you in London."

"Perhaps they will frighten me," Cheryl suggested.

"They will admire you!" Andrina said firmly.

She looked a little apprehensively at her sister as she spoke.

Cheryl was easily frightened by people, and on any social occasion Andrina was always very careful to keep beside her and prevent her from being upset.

Cheryl was extremely sensitive, and if one of the local Dowagers was rather brusque she would feel that she was being snubbed and would want to creep away from the party unnoticed.

"You are going to be a success in London," Andrina said now, "a big success, Cheryl! You will be the 'belle' of every Ball, feted and acclaimed! Every man you meet will want to lay his heart, his name, and his fortune at your feet!"

Cheryl did not answer, she merely looked rather anxious, and Andrina was glad when Sharon returned with a copy of *The Ladies' Magazine* in her hand.

She threw herself down in her seat at the table.

"Listen to this," she said. "It is written by Henry Luttrell:

> *"All on that magic List depends;*
> *Fame, fortune, fashion, lovers, friends:*
> *'Tis that which gratifies or vexes*
> *All ranks, all ages, and both sexes.*
> *If once to Almack's you belong,*
> *Like monarchs, you can do no wrong;*
> *But banished thence on Wednesday night,*
> *By Jove, you can do nothing right."*

There was silence for a moment after she had finished.

"Supposing we are banished?" Cheryl asked in a frightened voice.

"We will not be," Andrina replied positively. "If the Duke of Broxbourne cannot get us invited to Almack's, who can?"

"I hope you are right," Sharon said, "but, as I have already said, it depends entirely on the Patronesses, and whatever the Duke does or does not do, we will have to have a Chaperon."

"I have thought of that," Andrina replied. "That is something else the Duke will have to provide for us."

"Will we have to pay her?" Sharon asked.

Andrina was still for a moment.

"I hope not," she said at length. "That is something I did not take into consideration."

"But there should be enough money when we have sold the necklace. Where is it?"

"It is in Mama's bed-room where I looked at it last night," Andrina answered. "I knew where she had hidden it, and I left it there after she died just in case Papa should take it into his head to lay his hands on it."

She met Sharon's eyes, but neither of them said any-thing.

They both knew that their father in the last years of his life had been increasingly querulous and resentful of the poverty which prevented his enjoying many of the luxuries which he began to crave.

He wanted food such as could not be bought in their small village, and anyhow if they had shopped in Ches-ter it would have been much too expensive.

He demanded the best wine, and the only port and claret he considered worth drinking were well beyond their means.

Andrina pandered to him, coaxed him, and per-formed miracles with what little money she had to spend on the housekeeping.

It meant that she and her sisters went without new gowns or made their own out of the cheapest materials and could seldom afford even pretty ribbons with which to trim what they had made.

It meant too that they had to take turns in riding the only horse they could now keep in the stable.

It was an animal which also had to pull the carriage if their father wished to go driving, or the gig, which was more convenient for them to use themselves.

The garden was sadly neglected, and they were fortu-nate in having old Sarah, who had been with them since their childhood, to cook and do the rough work in the house.

The rest they shared amongst themselves.

Now it seemed to Andrina as if the gloom of those last years of her father's life was moving away from the house like a dark cloud that had encompassed them for far too long.

Even now she would sometimes wake in the night thinking she heard her father's hoarse voice calling her, demanding things she could not provide and finding fault with everything she did or tried to do for him.

"There is only one thing," Sharon said suddenly as they went up the stairs towards their mother's bed-room.

"What is that?" Andrina asked.

"Do you not think people in London will expect us to be in mourning? We have not been wearing black because we could not afford new clothes, and who was to see us living here except a few neighbours who understood our circumstances? But in London?"

"I have thought of that," Andrina answered. "Who is to know in London when Papa died? If anyone asks us, we will say that he died a year ago, and you know he would be the last person to expect us to walk about looking like black crows!"

"It is not so much a matter of what we look like," Sharon said. "But if we were to go to Balls wearing mourning, people would think it very reprehensible."

"Then they must not know we are in mourning," Andrina said. "It is as easy as that, and, Cheryl, do remember what I told you. Papa died last February, not this."

"I will remember," Cheryl promised, but Andrina knew she would have to remind her not once but a dozen times.

It was always difficult to know what Cheryl was thinking about. She was so quiet, sweet, and amenable; she seemed to live in a fantasy world of her own which had little or no contact with everyday life.

She looked so lovely that it was hard for people, once they had met her, to realise she made little contribution to the conversation, or that nothing she said, if she did speak, was worth remembering.

Now as she moved across the bed-room at the front of the house which had been their mother's she looked like an angel who had dropped out of Heaven by mistake.

Andrina took a chair and standing on it put up her hand to the top of the wardrobe.

"So that is where Mama hid the necklace!" Sharon exclaimed.

"It was quite safe there," Andrina answered. "Papa was not well enough during the last years of his life to climb up on a chair, and Sarah is too old to dust so high."

She lifted down a leather box as she spoke, and taking it to the window opened it so that the sunshine would glitter and shimmer on the necklace, which was Indian in design.

The filigree gold was very intricate and it was set with small rubies, a number of pearls which ornamented it like a fringe, and in the centre of the necklace there was a large emerald flanked by two smaller ones.

"It is very pretty," Sharon said, "but somewhat barbaric-looking!"

"That is why Mama never wore it," Andrina replied. "Papa brought it back with him from India where he had served under General Wellesley, who later became the Duke of Wellington."

She looked at the necklace and smiled.

"It was so like Papa to bring home something that was really quite useless. Mama told me once that she tried it with all sorts of gowns, but it looked out of place and she did not like to offend Papa by saying so."

"Papa liked everything that was exotic," Sharon said, and her voice did not make it sound very complimentary.

"I think really he liked things that were spectacular and unusual," Andrina explained. "That is what he wanted to be himself, and it was very frustrating for him to have no money and to have to settle down here."

"Why did it have to be Cheshire?" Cheryl asked.

Andrina smiled.

"You must know the answer to that, Cheryl, you have heard it often enough. Papa had won this house on the turn of a card, and when he gambled away his fortune, this was the only thing he had left."

"I had forgotten," Cheryl replied indifferently.

"But we have been happy here," Andrina said in a voice that made it sound as if she was trying to convince herself. "We have all been together and it is only

the last few years after Mama died that things have
been so different."

"Because of Papa!" Sharon remarked. "I cannot pretend that I am not glad it is over."

"Nor can I," Andrina agreed, "but I feel rather
guilty. We ought to be mourning him and feeling unhappy."

"There is no point in pretending to each other,"
Sharon said briskly.

Andrina shut the lid of the jewel-box.

"Now, are we agreed that I should go to London immediately, find the Duke, and see what arrangement I
can make with him?"

"Of course," Sharon agreed, "but can we not come
with you?"

"I did think at first that we should all go together,"
Andrina answered. "Then I realised that would cost a
great deal of money and we simply cannot afford it—
not at the moment, when we still owe for Papa's fu-
neral."

"No, I understand," Sharon sighed.

"I suppose I could sit outside the coach," Andrina
said doubtfully, "which only costs three pence a mile
instead of five pence. But it would be very cold and, if I
arrived red-nosed and snuffling, the Duke might take a
dislike to me."

"Oh, of course you must sit inside," Sharon cried.
"And I believe you are expected to tip the coachman a
shilling and the guard, if he is going the whole way, will
want two and six pence!"

"It is not going to be cheap," Andrina said with a
little sigh, "and I think we may have to sell something
out of the house, although I do not wish to do that until
we absolutely are obliged to do so."

"Hugo said the other day," Cheryl interrupted unexpectedly, "that his father would like to buy the picture
of the horse in Papa's study."

"Cheryl! You have not been telling Hugo how hard
up we are?" Andrina asked sharply.

Cheryl looked guilty, then her blue eyes filled with tears.

"Of course it does not matter what you say to Hugo," Andrina said quickly before her sister could reply. "He naturally knows our circumstances, just as I am sure everyone in the neighbourhood realises we are penniless."

She did not speak bitterly, she merely stated a fact.

"Was it wrong of me, Andrina?" Cheryl asked.

"No, of course not, dearest!" Andrina said, putting an arm round her shoulders.

"You are not angry?" Cheryl enquired.

"I am never angry with you!"

Andrina kissed her sister and then to change the subject she said;

"Come and help me pack, girls. There is a Stage-coach passing through the village tomorrow which goes direct from Chester to London in twenty-eight hours. The sooner I see the Duke, the better!"

"You are very brave!" Cheryl said admiringly. "I am glad you do not want me to go with you."

"Supposing he says no?" Sharon asked.

"Then I shall have to think of another plan," Andrina answered firmly.

Her soft mouth was for the moment set in a hard line. She was more determined than she had ever been about anything in her whole life that Cheryl and Sharon should have a chance to shine in London.

"Their beauty must be appreciated by people who matter," she told herself, "not just a few fox-hunting Squires or some old cronies of Papa's who come to the house from time to time."

She was well aware, although she had never discussed it with her sisters, that in the neighbourhood the mothers of unmarried daughters made every possible effort to exclude the Maldon girls from any parties where they wanted their offspring to shine.

They also did not encourage their sons to visit the Manor House, and the young wives clung almost feverishly to their husbands when Cheryl or Sharon appeared.

This meant that invitations of any sort were few and far between. Andrina, smarting under the injustice of it, knew that nothing she could do or say would make any difference.

She only hoped that Cheryl, who was so sensitive, was not aware that women looked at her apprehensively and were always ready to repulse her tentative overtures of friendliness.

Sharon was very much tougher but she was very young.

Only Andrina realised that, just as for her the years had passed by since she was eighteen without her having one reputable suitor, exactly the same would happen both to Cheryl and Sharon unless something was done about it.

"I have got to persuade the Duke," she told herself, but she was well aware that she was relying on her father's gambling luck.

It was a gamble, a wild gamble, in which she was backing an absolutely outside chance.

There was no reason why the Duke should even remember the friend he had not seen for perhaps eighteen years, nor could he be interested in any goddaughter with whom he had never communicated.

If he had given her a Christening-cup or -bowl, there was certainly no sign of it in the very meagrely stocked silver-cupboard; and if he had given her anything else, Andrina was quite certain her mother would have mentioned it.

"When you are grown up, darling," she had said once to Andrina, "I must try to find someone who will bring you out and give you a Season in London."

She gave a little sigh.

"It would be so wonderful if you married somebody rich and important! Then you could find suitable husbands for the girls. I think Cheryl will grow up to be very beautiful!"

There could be no doubt about that.

Even at thirteen, when other girls were ungainly, either too fat or too thin, with spots on their faces or tiresome affectations, Cheryl had the same angelic countenance with which she had dazzled people as a baby.

Sharon, who was sixteen months younger, had always been alluring.

She was not only beautiful but also fascinating, and as they grew older Andrina noticed that people often turned from Cheryl's celestial beauty to the sparkling gaiety of Sharon, who always had something to say and always contrived to make anything she talked about sound amusing.

"I have to be successful for their sakes!" Andrina told herself as she packed the few clothes she possessed into a valise that she could carry herself.

Since porters meant extra tips, she decided that for the one night, or perhaps two, that she would have to stay in London, she could manage with two or three light gowns which could be covered when she went out with the travelling-cloak of Madonna-blue wool which they all wore from time to time.

In fact, like the Gunnings, they exchanged their clothes amongst themselves, and Andrina finally set out for London with four gowns, two of her own, one of Cheryl's, and one of Sharon's.

They had pooled their clothes, stockings, and bonnets so that Andrina could take the best.

Their mother's clothes also were still in the house, but somehow Andrina had never been able to bear the thought of wearing her things, since even to think of her was to experience again the misery and unhappiness they had all felt when she died.

For a long time it seemed as if the sunshine had gone out of their lives.

For Andrina, who had been nearest to her mother, it was almost agony to come downstairs and not hear her mother's voice calling her from the Drawing-Room, or to wait after she had gone to bed for her mother to come to her room and say good-night.

She had been no less beautiful than her daughters, but in a way that was peculiarly her own.

It was Mrs. Maldon who accounted for Andrina's straight little aristocratic nose, for the perfection of Cheryl's curved lips, and Sharon's heart-shaped face.

She had been fair, though not with the sparkling gold which made Cheryl's hair so outstanding. Andrina was sure that when her father and mother were young it would have been difficult to find a more handsome couple in the whole length and breadth of England.

She knew her father had always wanted a son, but until he became so ill and suffered so much pain he had been very proud of his beautiful daughters.

"You are the 'Three Graces,' my dears," he would say sometimes. "If I were the fellow who had to award an apple for the most beautiful, I have not the slightest idea which of you I should choose!"

"It would be Cheryl," Andrina had said once.

Her father had looked at his second daughter and then he said:

"I would agree with you if Sharon did not make me laugh. There is something very beautiful about laughter."

He had then looked across the table at Andrina.

"And you, Andrina, are the most like your mother and therefore the ideal that every man has in his heart when he seeks a wife."

It had been the most complimentary thing her father had ever said to her.

After that, during his illness, he had seemed to resent her trying to look after him, and at times she had thought he must hate her because she would not buy him the things he wanted.

But what was the point, she thought now, of worrying about Papa?

She had to concentrate on the two girls, she had to look after them. There was no-one else to do it.

They had gone with her to the Stage-coach, Sharon carrying her valise, because, as she said, she had a long way to travel and must conserve her strength.

They waited at dawn on the high road at the end of the village known as Bigger Stukeby although, as Sharon had often pointed out, it was not really any larger than Little Stukeby, which was three miles away.

It was a cold, rather blustery day and Andrina was glad of her travelling-cloak and the fact that she wore a warm jacket under it.

They had had a long discussion as to what Andrina should wear to go to London and it was Cheryl who had said unexpectedly:

"You will have to change into something smart before you meet the Duke. You cannot just arrive at his house creased from travelling and carrying your valise. Besides, he might think you had come to stay."

"I thought of that," Andrina said, "and I have the names of various Hotels that I heard Mama mention from time to time."

"Would they not be very expensive?" Sharon asked.

"I am sure they will," Andrina replied, "but I shall ask them for their very cheapest room. If they cannot provide me with one, I dare say they can recommend somewhere respectable that is not so dear."

It had all sounded very plausible, Andrina thought, when she was talking about it to her sisters, but when the Stage-coach started off she suddenly felt alone and rather frightened.

She had often been to Chester and she had been to Liverpool and Crewe on several occasions, but she had never been out of her own county since early childhood and London seemed a very long way away.

But for good or evil she had embarked on this plan to find husbands for her sisters, and when the Stage-coach had driven off, leaving Cheryl and Sharon waving at the halt, she had settled down and told herself that she must be calm and sensible.

For one thing, she could not afford to make mistakes.

She had, however, been lucky in finding an inside-seat, although there was the complement of seven passengers already on the outside.

The fellow-traveller sitting opposite her she saw was

a middle-aged, tight-lipped, grey-faced man who looked like a Lawyer or Solicitor's clerk.

There was a stout farmer's wife beside her, taking up more than her fair share of the seat. She had a large basket covered with a white cloth which got in the way of everyone's feet and opposite her was a woman with a squalling child who appeared to resent travelling and intended to express his dissatisfaction vocally.

Andrina settled herself comfortably, although she found her valise somewhat cumbersome.

The guard on the coach had wished to put it outside, but she had resisted this suggestion because it contained the precious necklace which had belonged to her mother.

She was well aware that anyone who travelled by coach was always in danger of accidents, especially on a long journey.

The coach could be overturned by reckless driving or a drunken coachman, there were often reports in the newspapers of horses galloping off without drivers, or of travellers who bribed them in order to race another vehicle, with disastrous results.

Andrina did not intend to be separated from her valise.

At the same time, she had thought the coachman, in a many-caped overcoat with large, platter-like mother-o'-pearl buttons, looked a sober, sensible sort of man, and the four horses pulling the vehicle were in good trim.

She had often heard criticism expressed about the iniquity of the overloading of the Stage-coaches, and the cruelty inflicted on the animals who pulled them.

"I suppose you realise," one of her father's hunting friends had said severely a year ago, "that the average life of a horse pulling a coach at about eight miles an hour is six years, while at ten miles and over a horse lasts only three!"

"Something should be done about it!" Colonel Maldon said feebly.

"That is what I have said for a long time," his friend

answered, "and there have been a lot of letters in *The Times* and *The Morning Post*. But what do people care so long as they get to their destinations quickly and safely?"

"All I hope is that I never have to ride in a Stage-coach again," Andrina's father had said positively.

"I have never been in one, thank God!" his friend replied, "but with taxes increasing as they are, it will not be long before I shall have to take my place with the other paupers!"

He had snorted before he said angrily:

"Do you realise the tax on a two-wheeled private carriage is now seven pounds and on a four-wheel twenty-one pounds? And that is not counting the tax of five pounds on one horse and nine pounds on three! It is anarchy, that is what it is! And what does the Government do with the money, I ask you? They waste it!"

"That is true enough," Colonel Maldon had agreed.

"We are being taxed out of existence," his friend had said, and Andrina had found it difficult not to agree with him.

At the same time, she could not help wishing as the journey progressed that she had been able to travel in the comfort of her own carriage, as so many Cheshire families did when they were proceeding to London.

The clerk opposite her fell asleep and snored, the baby screamed, and the fat farmer's wife inched further and further towards Andrina. What was more, she ate continually of the food she had stored away in her covered basket.

It was quite fascinating to see how much she had brought with her.

There was a large pork-pie, slices of cold ham, hard-boiled eggs, and at least a dozen pasties, all of which she consumed one after another without offering a bite to anyone else in the coach.

Andrina was extremely glad when they stopped at about noon for luncheon at a Posting-Inn.

The landlord was expecting them, and a rather indifferent meal was slapped down in front of the coach-travellers, who were not considered to be very good customers.

There was, however, a hot soup, which, although not very appetising, was warming, and Andrina found that the excellent local cheese was more palatable than the slices of tough meat and badly cooked brawn that were served with watery vegetables.

They hardly had time to finish their food before they were off again, and now, although they stopped to change horses, the passengers were not expected to alight until they reached Leicester, where they were to stay the night.

Andrina closed her eyes and wondered if she would sleep a little, but the horses galloped and the coach swayed from side to side on the rough roads, and almost immediately the baby started crying again.

The farmer's wife only went a few miles before she again opened her food-basket, and now there was the pungent smell of onions, which apparently she found most appetising!

Andrina found it difficult to sleep because her mind was beset with the problems she would find when she arrived.

It had been one thing to tell the girls what she planned and sound confident, and quite another to beard an unknown Duke and try to make him feel that the three daughters of a long-lost friend were his special responsibility.

"Perhaps I ought to have brought Cheryl with me," Andrina told herself.

However old the Duke might be, unless he was completely blind, he would have been beguiled and astonished by Cheryl's beauty.

But Andrina had the feeling that Cheryl would not be much use under such circumstances.

If the Duke protested in any way about doing what was asked of him, Cheryl would immediately be hurt, and would capitulate and accept his refusal without protest.

Andrina had every intention of protesting, arguing, and begging until she got her own way.

"I intend to have no feelings concerning myself in the matter," she told herself. "If he thinks me audacious, he must just think so; if he thinks it impertinent, well, it will not worry me. All that matters is that he should agree."

In the afternoon there were storms: the rain beating against the closed windows made it impossible to look out.

Then it grew dusk and Andrina, like everyone else, began to think about dinner.

It was usual for the passengers of a Stage-coach to dine at about six o'clock, but it was after seven before they rumbled into a large Posting-Inn outside Leicester.

Andrina stepped out carrying her own valise, feeling stiff, crumpled, and in need of fresh air.

It had been cold sitting in the coach, and the smell of onions combined with the screams of the baby had made it intolerable.

A mob-capped maid showed her to the top floor of the Inn, where the very worst rooms were kept for Stage-coach passengers.

As they passed through the vestibule and climbed the stairs Andrina heard loud laughter and the noise of many voices coming both from the Tap-Room and the Dining-Saloon.

"You seem to be very crowded," she said to the maid walking ahead of her.

"It's the races, Miss. We're full right up and there's not another corner where you could put an extra mouse!"

Andrina smiled, then she said:

"It must mean a lot of extra work for you."

"The gentry tips well," the girl answered, "though I don't mind telling you, Miss, my feet feels as if they don't belong to me by the time I gets to bed!"

"I am sure they do," Andrina said, "but try putting a little mustard in hot water and soaking them. That helps."

"I never thought of that!" the girl exclaimed. "Thank you, Miss, I'll remember what you said."

Perhaps it was because Andrina had been so friendly that she was shown into an attic-room where she would sleep alone.

The fat farmer's wife and the woman with the crying baby were given a double-room to share next door, and Andrina was thankful she did not have to be with either of them.

She took off the gown in which she had travelled and hung it up on the back of the door. Then she washed herself and put on a velvet dress which she often wore at home.

It was a very pretty shade of crimson and had a lace collar and lace cuffs on the short, puffed-sleeves. Although it was not by any means fashionable, as Sharon had pointed out to her, it was warm and, although Andrina did not think about it, extremely becoming.

She tidied her hair and went downstairs, feeling, she told herself, ready to eat an ox, she was so hungry.

She found the landlord outside the Dining-Saloon, from which the noise appeared to have grown louder since she last passed it.

"Will you please show me to the table reserved for the Stage-coach passengers?" Andrina asked.

"The Stage-coach passengers?" the landlord repeated. "You'll be lucky if you get anything to eat before ten o'clock. All the tables are booked. We can't accommodate you until the gentlemen have finished!"

"But that is disgraceful!" Andrina said, annoyed not only by the information but also by the manner in which he spoke to her.

"You know as well as I do," she went on, "that the Inns are under an obligation to feed the Stage-coach passengers. Their meals, like their rooms, are reserved for them."

"I can't do the impossible!" the landlord retorted surlily. "You'll get your dinner when there's a place for you, and not before!"

"I consider it quite outrageous!" Andrina said sharply, then realised that the landlord was not even waiting for her comments, but had walked away from her down the passage.

"What is outrageous?" a cultured voice asked.

She turned to see a tall, broad-shouldered gentleman who had just come out of the door behind her so that she was blocking his way.

Because she was so angry Andrina, with her eyes flashing, told him the truth.

"The Stage-coach passengers, Sir," she replied, "are not to be fed until ten o'clock or later! We have been travelling all day and naturally we are extremely hungry!"

A burst of laughter from the Dining-Saloon almost drowned her last words.

The gentleman to whom she was speaking glanced over her head at the glass doors before he asked:

"I can perhaps understand the landlord's predicament when he has so many extra customers. Are you alone?"

"If you mean am I travelling without a personal companion," Andrina answered. "I am."

"Then may I, as an alternative to your waiting until ten o'clock, suggest that you dine with me?"

Andrina stiffened.

Her lips opened, ready to refuse, but the gentleman quickly said:

"It may perhaps seem rather unconventional, but I should imagine it would be more pleasant than waiting for two and a half hours, when doubtless any dish in the place that is worth eating will be off the menu."

He spoke in a sarcastic manner which Andrina found amusing, and she thought too, as she looked up at him, that he was obviously a gentleman of distinction and had a presence that was unmistakable.

His coat was exquisitely cut, his white cravat tied in intricate folds was spotless, and he had obviously changed for dinner.

Because she was in fact so hungry, Andrina made up her mind.

"Thank you, Sir," she said. "If you are quite certain it will not inconvenience you, I should be very glad to accept your invitation."

"As a matter of fact you will be doing me a favour," he said. "The friend who should have been with me decided to return to London when the racing was over. Will you come into my private Parlour?"

He made a gesture with his hand as he spoke. Then as Andrina walked ahead of him he turned to say to the Inn-keeper, who had reappeared:

"The bell appears to be broken! I have been ringing for the wine I ordered. Bring two bottles, and double the order for dinner."

"Very good, Sir," the landlord said in a very different tone of voice from that in which he had spoken to Andrina.

The gentleman turned and walked into the Parlour, where Andrina was already warming herself in front of a large log-fire.

The light there was brighter than that in the passage and she saw that she had not been mistaken in thinking he looked distinguished.

He was perhaps not handsome, but his high-bridged nose was aristocratic, his dark eyes had a rather quizzical look, and there was a twist to his lips which gave him a somewhat sardonic appearance.

"Shall we introduce ourselves?" he asked as he approached Andrina.

Andrina hesitated, thinking that perhaps it would be wiser not to give him her real name.

"My name is Morgan, Sir," she replied, "Miss Morgan."

"And mine is Sir Tancred Wensley."

Andrina dropped him a small curtsey and he bowed, slightly superciliously, she thought.

"You are really travelling alone, Miss Morgan?"

There was something in the way he said the words which made Andrina feel for the first time since she had met him a little self-conscious.

"There was unfortunately no-one who could accompany me," she replied.

"Then it is my good fortune that I can be of service to you," Sir Tancred said. "Will you not sit down, and may I offer you a glass of madeira?"

"Thank you," Andrina replied, "but only a very little, if you please. My father always said it was a great mistake to drink on an empty stomach."

"It is one of those wise adages with which I concur in theory, but break on every possible occasion!" Sir Tancred said lightly.

He poured Andrina a little of the madeira and brought it to her as she settled herself on one side of the hearth.

He took the other side, and she knew he was looking at her with his dark eyes, which she felt were almost impertinently searching and inquisitive.

After a moment he remarked:

"You are far too attractive, Miss Morgan, to be unattended."

"I assure you, I am quite safe with my fellow-travellers," Andrina answered with a smile. "They either snore, scream, or eat without ceasing!"

"But now you are not with them," Sir Tancred said.

She gave him a quick glance, then replied:

"If you feel it is imprudent of me, Sir, to have accepted your invitation, perhaps I had better wait until ten o'clock."

"I was not suggesting anything of the sort," Sir Tancred said. "I was merely thinking that to enter a Dining-Room, containing as it does a very mixed company from the race-course, would be far more dangerous for you than anything you will encounter here with me!"

"I am grateful for the reassurance," Andrina said primly.

As she spoke she realised that he was right and it might have been very unpleasant to go into the Dining-Saloon amongst a number of men who, she was quite certain from the noise and laughter, were speedily becoming "foxed" after a long day at the races.

But it would also not be very pleasant to go to bed without having eaten, and she could in fact feel nothing but gratitude to the gentleman who had seen her predicament. At the same time, she felt somewhat guilty about her fellow-travellers.

Then she told herself that the fat farmer's wife would certainly not be hungry, and the woman with the baby had not gone out of her way either to apologise for the noise he was making, or to make herself pleasant to anyone else on the coach.

She realised that Sir Tancred was waiting as if he expected her to make some comment, but at that moment the door opened and a mob-capped maid entered, bearing plates and dishes on a tray, and was followed by a waiter with wine and glasses.

Because she was in fact so hungry Andrina could not help her eyes lighting up.

"Here is our food!" she exclaimed, almost as if it were a miracle.

"I told you that you were wise to accept my invitation," Sir Tancred said. "So let us sit down and enjoy ourselves, and let me assure you once again, Miss Morgan, I am really very much obliged to you."

Andrina laughed.

"That is unfair!" she said. "That is what I should be saying to you, and now you have taken the words out of my mouth!"

He smiled and when she seated herself at the table he sat down in a high-backed chair which seemed to suit him.

Despite his air of distinction there was a casualness about him, in the way he moved and in the way he spoke, which made Andrina think he was unlike any man she had met before.

She told herself, as she glanced at him surreptitiously while he was giving orders to the waiter, that he was used to commanding.

At the same time, she felt that he would be a difficult

man to cross, and there was something slightly over-
bearing, or perhaps the right word was "autocratic,"
about him.

'Perhaps he has been a soldier,' she thought to herself, because in some ways he made her think of some
of the soldiers who called on her father during the War.

They had all had that same air of authority as if they
were ready to order the world round and expected to be
obeyed.

Watching Sir Tancred, Andrina told herself that she
was quite sure he had been a soldier and he was the
same type of man that Wellington must be.

The Hero of Waterloo had always been a man she
greatly admired and she would make her father tell her
over and over again of what he had been like when he
had fought under him in India.

"Only Wellington—or rather Wellesley, as he was
then—could have won the Battle of Assaye," her father
had said over and over again, "and only Wellington
could have made a success of the Peninsular War."

Her father had been very ill when the Battle of
Waterloo the previous year had brought a decisive end
to the Eleven Years' War.

Andrina had read him all the reports in the newspapers, and when they praised the "Iron Duke" and the
manner in which he had conducted the campaign,
Colonel Maldon had been able to forget for a little
while the pain he suffered.

The first course was the inevitable Mulligatawny
soup, which was a faithful stand-by not only in every
Inn but also in every private house.

Sir Tancred tasted it and reached for the pepper-mill,
but Andrina was too hungry to be particular.

She finished her plateful of soup without speaking,
then realised that Sir Tancred was sitting back in his
chair regarding her with a faint smile on his lips.

"Now tell me about yourself," he said. "I admit to
being somewhat intrigued."

CHAPTER TWO

Andrina had no intention of discussing her private affairs with a stranger, although she was sure that Sir Tancred could, if he wished, tell her much of what she wanted to know about the Duke.

She was certain that he was of Social consequence, perhaps one of the Regency Bucks of whom Sharon was always talking.

After a moment, as he was obviously waiting for her answer to his question, she replied:

"I am going to London."

"And what do you intend to do when you get there?" he asked.

"I am looking for a man," she replied truthfully.

Because she was intent upon helping herself to the next course, she was unaware that he raised his eyebrows and there was an amused twinkle in his eyes.

"That should not be difficult," he remarked.

"No, I am sure it will be quite easy!" Andrina replied.

She had made the same answer to Cheryl last night when her sister said:

"London is a big place, Andrina. How will you find the Duke when you get there if we do not know his address?"

"That will not be difficult," Andrina had answered. "There are not very many Dukes and someone will be able to tell me where his house is."

"Nearly all the Nobility have houses which bear their

names," Sharon interposed. "The Duke of Richmond lives at Richmond House, the Marquis of Londonderry lives at Londonderry House, and the Earl of Derby at Derby House."

"So the Duke of Broxbourne will live at Broxbourne House," Andrina said. "I am certain it will be somewhere in the Mayfair area."

"You will have to hire a hackney-carriage from where the Stage-coach sets you down at the Central Coach Office in Lud Lane."

"I have thought of that," Andrina said. "It will be expensive, but if I try any other method of transport I might get myself lost."

"Of course," Sharon agreed, "and anyway, if you arrived on foot at Broxbourne House the servants might refuse to let you see the Duke."

This was something which had already worried Andrina when she was making her plans.

If her father's description of the state and grandeur in which the Duke lived was true, there would be a whole army of servants to get by before she actually reached his presence.

Then she told herself that they would perceive she was a lady, and if she insisted, it would not be possible for them to prevent her from gaining access to their Master.

"What made you decide on this—adventure?" her dinner-companion asked.

There was a slight pause before the last word, but Andrina had made up her mind not to discuss her private affairs any further.

She certainly did not wish to talk about Cheryl or Sharon until she had convinced the Duke how important it was that they should be launched in Society, and it was impossible for her to talk about herself without including them.

Instead she said with a smile:

"Will you not tell me about the races? I know a little about horses and I should be interested to hear what won."

It was true that she knew the names of the best-known horses in the racing world.

Her father, in the last year of his life, suffered with his eyes and Andrina, or one of his other daughters, read aloud the newspapers to him every day.

Colonel Maldon had taken not only the *Morning Post* but also a sporting-paper which devoted itself mostly to racing and boxing.

The reports of the Mills and the injuries suffered by the pugilists taking part made Andrina feel slightly sick. But she enjoyed reading about horses racing and her father, if he was in a good mood, would tell her stories of the owners whom he had known when he was young.

She therefore managed to have quite an intelligent conversation with Sir Tancred, who seemed surprised that she knew so much.

"Are you an owner, Sir?" Andrina enquired.

"I am!" he answered.

He did not seem anxious to mention his horses by name and she thought perhaps he was one of those who were unfortunate on the turf and therefore he did not wish to speak of his losses.

When dinner was over and Andrina had refused a glass of port, Sir Tancred suggested that they move nearer to the fire.

"It was cold enough racing today," he said, "and this Inn, being old, seems to let in all the draughts."

"Perhaps you have not lived in the country as I have," Andrina said with a little smile. "One becomes immune to cold after a time."

She thought how cold the Manor House was during the winter. The snow had often blocked the roads and even to get to the village someone had to dig them out.

"You do not look the hearty type of country girl who would enjoy a breezy walk on the moors," Sir Tancred said with a twist of his lips. "I expect in London you will find someone who will be only too ready to wrap you in sables and fill your rooms with hot-house flowers."

There was something in the way he spoke which told Andrina he was being sarcastic.

She certainly did not expect the Duke to wrap her in sables. At the same time, there was no reason why any gentlemen she met at a Ball should not send her, and certainly Cheryl and Sharon, bouquets of flowers.

There was something about Sir Tancred which made her decide he was conceited.

He had a superior air, as if he thought he was better and of more consequence than anyone else.

'Perhaps that is only because he thinks I am insignificant and of no importance,' Andrina thought.

She wished she could make him see that she was not half as humble in origin as her clothes might suggest.

"People take you at face-value," her father had once said bitterly, "or rather at the value of your bank-balance!"

There must be some truth in this, Andrina thought.

If she were a lady of fashion, she was sure Sir Tancred would be paying her compliments and certainly not looking at her in a manner which made her feel shy.

Instead of sitting down beside the fire she said:

"I think, Sir, as the Stage-coach will be leaving very early in the morning—at five o'clock, to be precise—I should retire now. It has been a long day."

It had in fact been half past five when she boarded the Stage-coach, which had left Chester at five. The warmth of the fire, the big dinner she had eaten, and the glass of claret which Sir Tancred had persuaded her to drink was making her feel very sleepy.

"Thank you very much for giving me dinner," Andrina said. "It was exceedingly kind of you. I should have been very hungry indeed if I had had to wait until now, as the landlord intended."

"I see no reason for you to leave me so quickly."

Sir Tancred put his glass of port down on a side-table by the arm-chair and said:

"You are very pretty. If you are in search of a man, why go further?"

As he spoke he put his arms round Andrina and pulled her against him. Then as she was immobile with the surprise of his action, his lips were on hers.

For a moment the shock of realising he was kissing her made her unable to move, unable to struggle.

His lips were hard and demanding and the feel of them was different from anything Andrina had imagined a kiss would be like.

Then as she tried to move her hands to push him away a sudden sensation ran through her body, almost like a streak of lightning.

It was almost painful in its intensity and yet at the same time a rapture. Then before she could realise it was there or even think of it she tried to force herself away from him.

But she had not sufficient strength, as Sir Tancred held her completely captive, his mouth imprisoned hers, and his arms encircled her whole body so that she could not move.

Then instinctively, as Andrina realised what was happening and knew she must be free, she brought her heel down hard on Sir Tancred's foot.

He gave an exclamation that was half an oath and in that moment she twisted herself out of his arms and ran across the room towards the door.

As she opened it she was aware that he had not followed her, and in a voice which she hoped was cold and scathing but instead was somehow soft and breathless she said:

"I thought . . . I was dining with a . . . gentleman!"

She went out through the door and slammed it behind her.

She ran up the creaking oak stairs to the attics, hurried into her room, and, having lit a candle, locked the door behind her. Then she sat down on the bed to realise in consternation what had happened.

She had been kissed! Kissed for the first time in her life, by a man she had never seen before.

There had been quite a number of men from time to time who had tried to kiss Andrina, the sons of local

Squires, the elderly cronies who came to see her father and had an eye for a pretty girl, and on one memorable occasion a Member of Parliament.

He was a married man with four children, who pretended, when Andrina protested indignantly, that he was merely interested in her as a constituent.

The nearest anyone had ever got to kissing her was a light brush on her cheek, and she had been determined in her own heart that she would never give her lips to a man unless she loved him.

She was not quite certain what was implied by the immorality of which so many people spoke when they criticised the behaviour of the Regent and those who constituted the "Carlton House Set."

But she was sure it had something to do with kissing and she thought that to be kissed by a man one did not love or intend to marry would be to degrade one's self.

But now it had happened to her, and she had not thought that a kiss would be not only so intimate, but also, in a strange manner, disturbing.

It was impossible not to think of the strange feeling, half pleasure, half pain, that had run through her when Sir Tancred's mouth was on hers.

Had he been aware of it too? she wondered.

Then she told herself that his feelings in the matter were not of the least consequence.

He had behaved absolutely outrageously, not only in asking an unchaperoned and defenceless woman to dine with him, but then by insulting her.

She wished now that she had had the time to tell him exactly what she thought of his behaviour; but she had wanted to escape and she knew now how strong he was. If he caught her again she might not be able to free herself a second time.

She only hoped, she thought, that she had really hurt him when she had stamped on his foot.

Because it had been so cold she had worn not only her velvet evening-gown that was in no way décolleté, but she had also put on a pair of leather house-slippers,

strapped across the instep and on which there was a
well-shaped wooden heel.

It was undoubtedly quite an effective weapon when
used to good purpose!

"I hope it hurts him all night!" Andrina said almost
vindictively.

Then once again she remembered the strange feeling
his lips had evoked in her.

It had all happened so quickly and even now the
shock of finding Sir Tancred's arms round her and his
mouth on hers seemed like an illusion rather than reality.

But it had happened!

"Never again," Andrina told herself, "will I ever be
able to say I have never been kissed!"

Then as she thought about what had happened, she
realised that Sir Tancred had insulted her more than by
a kiss.

"If you are in search of a man, why go further?"

It had never occurred to her that her innocent answer to his question could be misconstrued into something unspeakable.

But it had, and Sir Tancred had thought . . . what
had he . . . thought?

Andrina felt her cheeks burning at the explanation
she could not express even to herself.

"How dare he?"

She said the words out loud.

"How dare he think such things!"

She wanted to scream at him, to strike him; and she
only wished she could have dug a sword into his foot
instead of using her heel.

Then she told herself firmly that it was no use getting
hysterical: she would never see Sir Tancred again, and
she would not give him the importance of even thinking
about him.

He was utterly and completely despicable!

*   *   *

There was, predictably, no sign of Sir Tancred the
following morning when the Stage-coach left the Inn at

five o'clock after a badly cooked and very sparse breakfast served by a yawning waitress.

The horses, however, were fresh and they made good progress on the journey to the next Posting-Inn, so that Andrina began to hope that she would arrive in London in time to see the Duke that night and not have to wait until the morrow.

Although she had sounded confident about finding accommodation at an Hotel, she was not so naïve as not to be aware that most Hotels would not welcome an unattached woman, especially one who was demanding the cheapest accommodation.

The hours passed slowly but the day was fine and the roads from Leicester were far better than those they had travelled on the day before.

The coachman also was obviously anxious to reach his destination. He pushed his horses, allowing the passengers the minimum amount of time at the Posting-Inns before he had them back in their places and they set off once again.

It was a great relief when the woman with the baby got off at Market Harborough and her seat was taken by an elderly red-faced man who appeared to have fortified himself against the journey.

After a few jovial remarks to the assembled company he put a large bandana handkerchief over his face and went to sleep, snoring louder than the clerk who was still sitting opposite Andrina had done the day before.

Without mishap, without check of any sort, they rolled into the yard of the *Swan with Two Necks* in Lud Lane, which was off Gresham Street, on the stroke of five o'clock.

The yard was much bigger than Andrina had expected and seemed to seethe with activity. She had never seen so many coaches or horses together before.

She expressed her thoughts aloud and the fat man in the furthest corner replied:

"Aye, William Chapter knows his job right enough! Thirteen hundred horses he had when Oi last asked he, and sixty coaches on road!"

The cold and bleary-eyed travellers from the incoming coaches untangled their aching limbs and hastened to the coffee-room.

Waiting passengers finished their pigeon-pies, boiled beef and ham, and took a last nip of brandy before taking their places in the out-going vehicles.

Remembering what Cheryl had said about making herself presentable, Andrina went at once to the *Swan with Two Necks* and asked if it was possible to hire a room where she could change her clothes.

"It'll cost yer two shillings," the porter said laconically.

"Two shillings?" Andrina exclaimed. "But I shall not be using it for more than ten minutes!"

"Two shillings is wot we charge," the porter said in a "take it or leave it" voice which told Andrina it would be stupid to argue.

"Very well," she said, producing the money, and he told the page-boy to show her into a small, badly furnished room at the back of the Inn.

She took off her travelling-gown and after washing herself put on a more elegant creation which the girls had decided was the best garment she had in which to confront the Duke.

It was passably fashionable since Andrina had taken in the skirt which had been much too full, heightened the waist, and added a frill of real lace around the neck which she had found in one of her mother's drawers.

The material was a soft pink which became her and, she thought, gave a little colour to her pale cheeks.

The bonnet she had worn during the journey had also been her mother's and it had been greatly improved by some ribbons that Sharon, who was quite skilful with her fingers, had sewn on it.

When she had finished dressing Andrina looked at herself in the mirror, and decided that, if nothing else, she looked a lady, and, without the competition of Cheryl and Sharon, she was as pretty, if not prettier than most of the women anyone would meet in London.

At least she hoped so, but now that she had reached the busy metropolis she was half afraid that what had seemed beautiful in Cheshire would pale into insignificance in the Social world.

Then she told herself that there was in fact no doubt that Cheryl and Sharon were beautiful and she herself was definitely pretty.

She would be a fool if she thought otherwise.

"Besides," Andrina told herself, "I shall never convince the Duke if I am not convinced myself."

She ordered a hackney-carriage and told the driver to go to Broxbourne House.

"In Curzon Street, Miss?" the man asked.

"That is correct," Andrina replied, only hoping it was.

Sharon had been right, she thought, as they set off. The great houses in London were called after their owners and naturally the drivers of the hackney-carriages would know where they were situated.

At the same time, as they drove along she could not help a cold feeling inside her which seemed to increase as they came to what was obviously the more fashionable part of the city.

There were a number of large, imposing Mansions and Squares in which the gardens in the centre were filled with the first flowering shrubs of spring.

There were lilacs, laburnums, and syringa, all more in bloom than the same shrubs were in their garden at home.

Andrina was sitting forward in her seat, watching the crowds in the streets, noting the carriages drawn by superlative horse-flesh, and feeling as if a new and exciting panorama was unfolding itself before her eyes.

"London is exciting!" she told herself.

She was absorbed in looking out the window, catching a glimpse of a hurdy-gurdy with a red-coated monkey on top, and surprisingly a flock of sheep being cursed by the drivers of drays piled high with barrels.

There were women with baskets selling bunches of primroses and daffodils, a muffin-man ringing his bell

and balancing on top of his head a tray filled with his
wares.

It was all fascinating to Andrina and it came as a
surprise when the carriage slowed down and she realised they were entering through high, wrought-iron
gates which were open to reveal at the end of a short
drive a large white Mansion.

Andrina had only a quick glimpse of flower-beds
planted with crimson tulips and the high white pillars of
a portico, before they had reached the front door and
footmen with powdered wigs and wearing elaborate
dark blue and gold-braided uniforms opened the door.

She stepped out and because she was very conscious
that her valise was on the seat beside her, with her travelling-cloak thrown over it, she decided that she must
be extravagant and tell the cabby to wait for her.

She was confronted on the doorstep by an exceedingly imposing, pontifical man who Andrina realised
was the Butler.

"Your pleasure, Madam?" he asked with a solemnity
she found slightly intimidating.

"I wish to see the Duke of Broxbourne."

"Have you an appointment with His Grace,
Madam?"

"No," Andrina answered. "Will you kindly inform
His Grace that I am here after travelling a long way,
and that my name is Miss Andrina Maldon, the daughter of Colonel Guy Maldon!"

She spoke slowly so that the Butler could take in
what she said, and she had rehearsed it to herself.

"Will you come this way, Madam?" the Butler asked.

He walked slowly, like the verger leading the choir
up the aisle in Church, Andrina thought.

She found herself in a large marble Hall decorated
with statues. A double staircase with gilded bronze
balustrading led up to the first floor, a huge crystal
chandelier hung from the ceiling, and there were a
number of gold-framed mirrors in which Andrina could
see herself reflected and rereflected.

There were also an inordinate number of footmen,

she thought, and because they made her feel shy, she
lifted her head a little higher and walked with her back
straight, as her mother had always taught her to do.

The Butler opened a large mahogany door.

"If you will wait here, Madam," he said, "I will inform his Grace of your arrival."

He shut the door behind Andrina and she looked
round her with an irrepressible curiosity.

The room was not large, but exquisitely furnished.
Never had she imagined she would see so many
treasures collected in one place.

She had visited some large and important houses in
Cheshire, but none of them had anything to compare
with the French Commodes she saw now, the inlaid
Secretaire, the high-back tapestry chairs.

There were pictures which she knew instinctively
were masterpieces, and the enamel and china orna-
ments were all, she was quite certain, priceless.

'I wish Papa had told me more about the Duke,' she
thought.

She understood now how impressed he must have
been with the Duke's house in the country if it had contained the same sort of furnishings she saw here.

But while he had told her about the Dining-Hall with
its gold candelabra and *Sèvres* china, the Salons magnificent and impressive, the Park, gardens, and stables,
he had never, as far as Andrina could remember,
described the Duke himself.

All she knew was that he must be very old since he
had not been a young man when her father had known
him, and that he had once been condescending enough
to become her godfather.

'I hope he is not too deaf to hear what I have to say,'
Andrina thought apprehensively.

It seemed to her now that all sorts of snags and difficulties presented themselves.

Supposing the Duke was bed-ridden?

She could hardly expect him then to sponsor three
young girls in fashionable Society.

Supposing he was not only deaf, but blind? That was something which had never occurred to her before.

If he was blind he could not appreciate the beauty of Cheryl and Sharon; therefore, half the point of what she had to say would be lost.

But it was too late now to have any hesitations. She had taken the first step and was not only in London, but actually inside Broxbourne House. That was an achievement in itself!

She realised that her fingers were trembling and her knees felt weak; so she sat down on one of the tapestry-covered chairs.

There was a clock on the mantelpiece which ticked noisily. There was a contemptuous sound about it, Andrina thought, and it had a superior sort of face, as if it felt she had no right to be there, forcing her way in where she was not wanted.

The clock ticked on—five minutes passed, ten, then fifteen.

Andrina wondered if they had forgotten her. Perhaps the Butler had gone to his pantry and it had escaped his memory that she was waiting.

She wondered how long she should remain where she was without reminding a footman at any rate of her presence.

Then she told herself that she was being absurd.

The Duke would not be sitting alone in Broxbourne House waiting for her to call. He might have friends with him.

He might be having a rest, or, on the other hand, he might be changing for dinner.

She looked apprehensively at the clock. It was ten minutes to six, and while some people in Cheshire still dined very early she was almost certain she remembered Sharon saying that the Prince Regent dined at seven, or had it been half-past?

The minutes ticked on. When at last Andrina was quite certain she had been forgotten, the door opened and the Butler said in a tone of one who passes judgment:

"If you will come this way, Madam, His Grace will see you."

Andrina rose to her feet and forced herself to walk slowly and with dignity as she followed the Butler across the Hall.

They went a little way down a wide passage and came to a door outside which stood two footmen on duty.

As the Butler and Andrina approached they opened the double mahogany doors simultaneously and the Butler announced in stentorian tones:

"Miss Andrina Maldon, Your Grace!"

Feeling as if she approached the guillotine, Andrina walked into the room.

Her first glance at the books reaching to the ceiling made her realise that it was a Library.

Then she was aware that a man was standing on the hearth-rug with his back to the mantelshelf.

She moved towards him, then suddenly stopped still!

For a moment she thought she must be dreaming or seeing things; for it was not an elderly man who stood there, but Sir Tancred Wensley!

There was complete silence and Andrina thought that Sir Tancred was as astonished as she was. Then, without choosing her words, she asked:

"What are you doing here?"

"I was just about to ask you the same question," he replied.

He was looking even more awe-inspiring than he had done the night before and Andrina realised it was because he was wearing evening-clothes.

The dark-blue satin evening-jacket with long tails accentuated the breadth of his shoulders, and his cravat, with the points of his collar high against his chin, was more intricately tied than it had been the previous evening.

Andrina's shyness at his appearance was swept away by a sudden anger as she remembered how he had behaved towards her.

She told herself swiftly that she had no intention of

allowing him to circumvent her in her determination to see the Duke.

"I asked to see the Duke of Broxbourne," she said, and was relieved to hear that her voice was well under control.

"So I understood," Sir Tancred replied, "but I am exceedingly surprised to discover that the Miss Morgan with whom I dined last night should have changed to Miss Maldon when she reached London."

Andrina had a sudden fear that he would tell the Duke what had occurred at the Posting-Inn.

It would be unlikely that anyone would believe she had not encouraged him, having agreed to dine alone with a man she had never met before.

She supposed that Sir Tancred was staying with the Duke, and she wondered frantically whether she would be wise to beg him to keep secret the fact that they had met before.

Then she thought it would only be a humiliating plea and he might refuse.

"Are you going to tell me why you are here?" Sir Tancred enquired.

"Certainly not!" Andrina replied. "I asked to see His Grace and when he appears I should be obliged if you would kindly leave us alone."

"You have something of a secret nature to impart to him?"

"What I have to say is private," Andrina replied, "and could be no possible concern of yours."

"But I am interested," Sir Tancred said, "and in case you are wondering, my foot is bruised and still somewhat painful!"

"I am delighted to hear it!"

"You are certainly adroit at getting yourself out of trouble. Perhaps you have had a great deal of practise?"

Andrina drew herself up proudly.

"I have no desire to discuss such matters," she said. "If you intend to stay in this room until His Grace appears, I suggest we wait in silence."

She found it difficult to speak crushingly when she was aware that Sir Tancred's eyes were twinkling and there was that cynical—or was it sardonic?—twist to his lips which she had noticed the previous night.

"Now suppose we stop fencing," he said after a moment, "and you tell me why you are here and what you want with me."

"With you?" Andrina retorted, "I have nothing . . ." She stopped suddenly.

A terrifying thought came to her.

As he saw her grey eyes widen in her small face, Sir Tancred, as if in answer to her unspoken question, said:

"I am the Duke of Broxbourne!"

"You? But how can you be?" Andrina demanded impulsively before she could stop to think. "His Grace is old . . . very old!"

"My father—to whom I imagine you are referring—died three years ago. A month in fact before his eightieth birthday!"

Andrina drew in her breath.

"But you said your name was Wensley," she said somewhat childishly.

"So it is! It is one of my titles which I frequently use when travelling!"

The Duke indicated a chair with a gesture of his hand.

"Will you not sit down, Miss Maldon?" he said. "Then perhaps you will tell me why you came to see me, or rather my father."

"How can he have died?" Andrina said almost to herself. "It is something I did not anticipate."

"It happens to all of us in time," the Duke remarked in a voice which made her think he was laughing at her.

"It may seem funny to you," she said aggressively, "but I had been so sure that he would be here and would listen to what I had to say to him."

"I am listening."

"But it would not be the same with you," Andrina said petulantly.

"Why not?" the Duke enquired.

"Because for one thing you are not my godfather," Andrina replied.

The Duke smiled.

"So you were one of Papa's many godchildren. I never understood why he so often accepted such a responsible position, seeing that he certainly made no effort to attend to their religious upbringing, and left them nothing in his will!"

"I was not expecting anything," Andrina said, "but I wanted his help, and I thought I could appeal to his better nature, or perhaps his conscience!"

The Duke threw back his head and laughed.

"That is the first time I have ever heard that my father had a conscience!" he said. "And as for his helping you, he was the most selfish man alive, with the possible exception of myself!"

Andrina twisted her fingers together, then she said in a very small voice:

"You do not consider, Your Grace, that your father's responsibilities have descended onto you?"

"In principle—no!" the Duke replied. "But I am prepared to hear the nature of his responsibility, Miss Maldon."

It was difficult—more difficult than Andrina had imagined it would be.

Try as she would, she could not help remembering that the man sitting opposite her had kissed her the night before.

It was disgraceful! It was outrageous! Something he should have never done!

She had hoped never to see him again, and yet by some terrible twist of fate he was the only person, she thought despairingly, who could help Cheryl and Sharon to make suitable marriages.

Unexpectedly the Duke said:

"As I am aware, you have been travelling since early this morning. You must be both tired and hungry. Let me offer you a glass of wine and perhaps some refreshment?"

"No, thank you," Andrina replied quickly. "I want to tell you why I am here and it is too important for me to think of anything else."

"It is of course impossible for me to guess what it could be," the Duke said.

He leaned back in his chair, very much at ease, and Andrina told herself that she hated him.

He was not making it easy for her, and now she realised how preposterous her suggestion was going to sound.

"My father . . . Colonel Guy Maldon . . . was a friend of your . . . father's," she began, "or rather . . . your father was kind to him when he was a young man. He used to stay at his . . . house in the country and he often . . . spoke about those days!"

She paused, wondering why it was so hard to speak, and her lips felt dry.

"Go on," the Duke prompted.

"My father lost his money . . . gaming," Andrina continued, "and after that he and my mother had to leave London and live in Cheshire where they had a house, and so they lost touch with their old friends."

"My father did not communicate with them in any way?"

"No," Andrina said.

"It is what might be expected. My father was neither loyal nor faithful to his friends. 'Out of sight—out of mind' was the usual way in which he treated them!"

"My father always spoke of yours with great affection," Andrina said, "and now that he is . . . dead, I thought perhaps the Duke might have remembered the days they spent together and that I was his godchild . . . and he would . . ."

Andrina's voice died away.

It was almost impossible to speak the words she had come to say with the Duke watching her and making her feel unaccountably nervous.

"What were you expecting him to do?" the Duke asked after a moment, when she did not seem inclined to go on.

"I wanted him to . . . introduce my sisters to . . . London Society," Andrina answered.

The words came out in a rush and as she spoke the colour rose painfully in her cheeks, moving from her small chin up to her large worried eyes.

"Introduce your sisters into Society?" the Duke repeated incredulously. "My father would never have entertained such an idea—he disliked Society! He had no use for it! And as for young women—I doubt if he ever spoke to one!"

"There is no-one else who can help," Andrina said in a low voice, "and Cheryl is beautiful, more beautiful than any girl you have ever seen, and Sharon is very beautiful too, but in a different way. They are exceptional, unique! Far lovelier than Elizabeth and Maria Gunning . . . and it seems so wrong, so unfair, that they should be buried in the country!"

"If my father had agreed to this extraordinary idea of yours, which I can assure you he would never have done," the Duke said, "were you suggesting that he should also pay for the privilege?"

There was a jeering note in his voice which made Andrina feel a hot wave of anger rise inside her. But she told herself it would be fatal to lose her temper, or to speak in anything but a polite and pleading tone.

"Certainly not!" she replied, but it was more defiant than polite. "We were perfectly prepared to pay our way!"

As she spoke she held out to the Duke the leather case which contained her mother's necklace.

She had taken it out of her valise at the *Swan with Two Necks* and had carried it with her in the hackney-carriage and when she entered the house.

"What is that?" the Duke enquired.

He made no effort to take the case from her and Andrina rose to her feet to cross the space between them and place it in his hands.

He opened the box and looked at the Indian necklace with surprise.

"My father brought it back from India," Andrina explained. "Mama kept it and would never sell it, however poor we were. I am sure that she intended to keep it to pay for Cheryl and Sharon's weddings when they got married."

She paused and then said distinctly:

"There will be no chance of their getting married or of meeting the right sort of prospective husband where we are living now. They must come to London!"

"And you think this will pay their expenses?" the Duke enquired.

"It is worth at least five hundred pounds," Andrina told him, "and if they could come up for this Season, just until June, they should be able to meet suitable young men."

"I see you have thought this out in some detail, Miss Maldon," the Duke said.

I am trying to make you understand how important it is for us," Andrina said.

"Us?" he questioned. "That is the first time you have included yourself in this grandiose scheme. I thought it was only your sisters who concerned you."

"I thought that ... I should be there to ... look after them and to ... guide them," Andrina faltered. "If they could ... manage without me ... then there would be no reason for me to stay in London."

"You are very self-effacing, Miss Maldon," he said, but it did not sound particularly complimentary.

"You do understand why I wanted to see your father," Andrina said pleadingly. "I felt perhaps he would realise he had . . . neglected an old friend who had fallen on hard times and might wish to make . . . amends by doing . . . something for his daughters."

"My father would not have considered himself under any obligation, morally or otherwise," the Duke replied. "If your father dropped out of circulation, he had only himself to blame."

There was silence, until Andrina said in a very low voice:

"You would not ... contemplate doing what I ... ask?"

"I certainly would not!" the Duke replied. "I am a bachelor, Miss Maldon, and I assure you I am far from being the right person to sponsor three débutantes—however attractive they may be!"

"There is one thing I . . . forgot," Andrina said.

"What is that?" the Duke enquired.

"There was a family connection between my father and yours. I think they shared a great-great-grand-mother. Anyway, my father sometimes spoke of the Duke as his cousin."

"What was the name of this great-great-grand-mother?" the Duke enquired, and Andrina was sure that he was sneering.

"Bentinck."

"It is certainly a name which appears in our family-tree," he conceded.

"Then it would not be as if you were helping complete strangers."

She knew she was being importunate by continuing to plead with him, and yet she felt as if all her plans had fallen flat like a card-castle.

There was something ignominious in knowing that, having come all this way to London, she must just turn round and go back.

She looked at the Duke's face and was quite certain that he was not only unmoved by her appeal but not even interested in what she had to say.

She had failed and the disappointment was like a stone heavy in her breast.

Taking from him the box which contained the neck-lace, she turned without speaking and walked towards the door.

"Where are you going?" the Duke asked.

"Home."

"At this hour?" the Duke asked sharply. "My dear girl, you cannot wander about in London alone."

"Your Grace need not be concerned," Andrina answered. "I can look after myself!"

"As you did last night?" he enquired.

She felt a surge of irresistible anger as she replied:

"You can hardly blame me for that!"

"Who else? When you were travelling alone without even a maid? And you told me you were going to London in search of a man!"

"I was not to know that Your Grace would misconstrue my words," Andrina began.

Her eyes were dark with fury as she added:

"How dared you think . . . what you thought? . . . It was inexcusable!"

"What could you expect me to think?"

"But you must have . . . known. Do I look as if I were . . . that sort of . . . woman?"

"My poor innocent," the Duke said scathingly, "pretty girls who have no wish to get into trouble do not travel alone, and never—do you hear me?—never do they accept invitations from strange men!"

The severity of his tone brought the colour once again into Andrina's face, and feeling utterly humiliated she turned once again towards the door.

"You are not to leave until you tell me where you intend to spend the night," the Duke ordered. "Surely you know someone in London?"

"I have never been here before," Andrina replied.

She wanted to run away, to hide herself somewhere! But she had the uncomfortable feeling that it would be impossible for her to go until he gave her permission to do so.

"Of all the scatter-brained, half-witted, idiotic ideas, yours is the worst!" the Duke stormed. "How could you have thought up anything so incredibly naïve, so foolish, so absurd?"

"I thought . . . your father would . . . help me," Andrina faltered. "I did not expect to . . . stay with him. I thought we could rent a house and . . . he would . . . find us a . . . Chaperon."

"The whole idea was mad from start to finish," the Duke said furiously. "A Chaperon indeed! Where do you think my father, or I for that matter, can find you a Chaperon, especially at this time of the night?"

"I am . . . going to an . . . Hotel."

"And what respectable Hotel would take in an unescorted woman, looking like you?" he asked.

"There must be . . . somewhere . . ."Andrina began desperately.

Now she was beginning to feel frightened.

London was very big, and even living in the country she had heard talk of the depravity in the city, although she had never expected to come in contact with it.

She looked very small, very young, and very pathetic as she stood halfway to the door, her eyes frightened, the colour the Duke had brought to her cheeks still vivid against the whiteness of her skin.

He stared at her and she thought from his expression that he disliked her as much as she disliked him.

Suddenly he put out his hand and tugged at the bell-pull.

"Come and sit down," he ordered. "I suppose I shall have to see what I can do about this."

The door opened before Andrina had time to obey him.

"Fetch Mr. Robson!" the Duke commanded.

"Very good, Your Grace."

Andrina sat on the edge of the chair she had previously occupied.

The Duke did not look at her but stood with his back to the fire, and she knew by the squareness of his chin and the tight line of his mouth that he was incensed.

After an uncomfortable two minutes the door opened and a middle-aged man with grey hair and what Andrina thought was a worried face came into the room.

"You wished to see me, Your Grace?"

"Yes, Robson," the Duke replied. "I require a Chaperon for this lady!"

"A Chaperon, Your Grace?"

"That is what I said."

"I am afraid I do not understand, Your Grace."

"Then let me make it clear," the Duke replied. "This is Miss Andrina Maldon, a distant cousin—very distant, but nevertheless a relative—and her father and mine were friends, if he ever had any friends!"

Mr. Robson made a polite bow to Andrina, which she returned.

"Miss Maldon informs me," the Duke went on in a lofty tone, "that since she is also my father's goddaughter, she considers it my duty to shoulder the responsibilities that my father lamentably neglected during his life-time and to introduce her two sisters and herself to Society."

Andrina gave an exclamation of sheer astonishment.

She looked up at the Duke and felt for a moment that her heart had stopped beating.

He had agreed! She had won!

She could hardly believe that she had actually heard him say the words!

"You will therefore appreciate, Robson," the Duke continued, "that the Misses Maldon must be provided with a Chaperon who is not only knowledgeable about such matters, but who will also be acceptable to the great hostesses."

"I understand, Your Grace, but it will not be easy," Mr. Robson said, and his expression was now even more worried than it had been before.

"I am well aware of that," the Duke said, "but I suppose such paragons do exist."

"There is Your Grace's Aunt—the Countess of Himley . . ." Mr. Robson began.

"An odious woman!" the Duke interposed. "I will have nothing to do with her. I cannot imagine how you can even mention her name!"

"I beg Your Grace's pardon."

There was silence as Mr. Robson appeared to be thinking, then suddenly he suggested tentatively:

"What about Lady Evelyn Lindsay, Your Grace? She is Your Grace's cousin, and you will remember that her late husband was Ambassador to Brussels. She must be finding it very dull living on his pension, and I am sure she would welcome the opportunity to return to the Society world in which she once shone so brightly."

"I knew you would not fail me, Robson!" the Duke said. "Lady Evelyn will do excellently. Take a carriage and fetch her here immediately!"

"Here, Your Grace? And immediately?"

"Miss Maldon will be staying and she must be Chaperoned."

"Yes, of course, Your Grace. I will leave at once. Lady Evelyn lives north of the Park in Dorset Square."

"Then fetch her, Robson," the Duke commanded.

The Secretary bowed and went from the room.

Andrina rose to her feet.

"What can I say?" she asked. "I never thought you would . . . agree. I am grateful . . . so overwhelmingly . . . whole-heartedly grateful!"

"Let me make this quite clear," the Duke said harshly. "I am embroiling myself in your crazy, senseless scheme against my better judgment, against every instinct and every inclination."

"But you have . . . agreed!" Andrina said breathlessly.

"I have agreed, God help me!" the Duke said. "But I wish to have as little part as possible in the whole inane business!"

"I will try not to . . . worry you," Andrina promised humbly, but her heart was singing.

CHAPTER THREE

Andrina felt as if she were living a dream.

She was so used to planning everything herself ever since her mother's death, and organising the household and her sisters, that she found it extraordinary to have everything arranged for her.

She realised the very evening she arrived that the Duke's life was organised in a most meticulous manner which proved, as the days passed, a continual surprise to her.

When she was upstairs changing for dinner and two housemaids were unpacking her valise, there was a knock on the door and an elderly woman in rustling black silk, who she realised must be the Housekeeper, came into the room.

"Mr. Robson would be very grateful, Miss, if you would let him know your home address, so that the coachman can plan the journey which he is to start at dawn tomorrow morning."

"Tomorrow morning?" Andrina asked.

"That is what I understood, Miss," the Housekeeper replied, "and I am to travel in the carriage so that I can look after your sisters on the return journey."

The Housekeeper would certainly be a very respectable and reliable escort, Andrina thought with a smile, realising that the Duke was determined to protect her sisters against finding themselves in the same reprehensible situation in which she had been involved.

Even to think not only of the way he had behaved

but also of the scathing manner in which he had spoken
about it made her feel a quick surge of anger.

At the same time, she could not help being glad and
excited by the thought that Cheryl and Sharon would
be with her quicker than she had anticipated.

"I am afraid it is a long journey for you to under-
take," she said to the Housekeeper.

"His Grace is sending a groom ahead to ask if we
can stay the night on the way back with Lord and Lady
Drayton, who have a house not far from Market
Harborough," the Housekeeper replied. "So we shall be
quite comfortable, Miss, and not have to put up in one
of those horrible Posting-Inns."

Because she could not repress her curiosity, Andrina
asked:

"I understand that His Grace sometimes stays in
them."

"So I believe," the Housekeeper said stiffly. "But His
Grace is very particular whose hospitality he accepts,
and Lord and Lady Drayton keep early hours and are
in fact a trifle old-fashioned."

'Cheryl and Sharon will certainly have no chance of
getting into any mischief!' Andrina thought.

She wrote down the address as the Housekeeper had
requested and scribbled a note to the girls, telling them
that everything was even better than they had hoped for
and she was waiting impatiently for their arrival.

She could imagine the excitement there would be
at the Manor House when they received her note.

In a way she was sorry that she could not be there
to tell them herself, but she was to learn that there
were a great many things for her to do in London.

When she had gone down to dinner wearing an evening-gown which she had fortunately brought with her,
she was feeling a little nervous of meeting Lady Evelyn
Lindsay.

The Duke had arranged to dine late, as Andrina realised, so that she would be properly Chaperoned.

It had never seemed to strike him, she thought, that
Lady Evelyn might, when Mr. Robson called for her,

have been out or might have had other plans. He behaved, she thought resentfully, as if the whole world
were just waiting to do his bidding!

When she entered the large Salon where the Butler
told her His Grace was waiting, it was to find him talking to a lady Andrina glanced at a little apprehensively.

She had been half afraid that the Chaperon chosen
for them by the Duke would be someone strait-laced
and haughty, rather like some of the Dowagers in
Cheshire who disapproved of Cheryl simply because of
her beauty.

But as she walked over the soft carpet towards the
hearth-rug she heard a light laugh and when she saw
Lady Evelyn much of her anxiety disappeared.

She must have been nearly sixty, but there was a
youthfulness about her slim figure and a light in her
eyes which proclaimed that she still enjoyed life.

She had never been beautiful, but she was smart and
fashionable in a manner which made Andrina immediately conscious of how inadequate her gown was.

She had copied it very carefully from a design in the
Ladies' Journal. But she had only been able to afford
the cheapest material, and although the colour became
her, there was no disguising the fact, she told herself
uncomfortably, that it looked home-made.

Lady Evelyn's gown, although, as Andrina realised
later in the evening, it was certainly not new and had in
fact seen a great deal of wear, proclaimed the magic
word "Paris" in every seam, in every ribbon, and in every movement of the narrow skirt.

Crossing the Salon, Andrina realised that the Duke's
eyes were on her face, and because he made her feel
shy she kept her own downcast until she reached his
side.

"Evelyn, may I present Andrina Maldon," he said to
the woman seated on the sofa. "She and her sisters have
a connection with our family through Great-Great-
Grandmother Bentinck, so of course they are not only
my cousins but also yours!"

Lady Evelyn held out her hand.

"Welcome to the family!" she said. "I can see at first glance that you are one of the most attractive assets we have had in centuries!"

Andrina curtseyed and Lady Evelyn drew her down beside her on the sofa.

"It is the most exciting thing that has ever happened!" she said. "That you and your sisters should have appeared from no-where and that Tancred should constitute himself your Guardian!"

She gave the Duke a sly glance from out of the side of her eyes and said:

"I cannot imagine what our relations will say, especially Louise, who has no fewer than five daughters whom you have never condescended to honour with a Ball!"

"A Ball?" Andrina asked, and found it hard to say the word.

"Of course," Lady Evelyn replied. "How better can Tancred and I present you to the *Beau Monde* than at a Ball? I believe the last one that took place in this house was over twenty years ago!"

Dinner in the huge Dining-Room, where they were waited on by half-a-dozen footmen and the pontifical Butler, was not the difficult meal that Andrina had feared as she came downstairs.

Lady Evelyn chatted gaily about friends and relations she and the Duke had in common, of what had happened in Brussels after Napoleon's abdication in 1814 when her husband had been Ambassador there, and a number of other subjects.

"Poor Herbert! If only he had not died before we had time to enjoy the peace," she said. "I was hoping that after Brussels we could have gone to Paris, the Mecca of all Diplomats, but it was not to be."

There was just for a moment a wistful note in her voice, then she went on:

"If a balloon had dropped down the chimney I could not have been more surprised, when Mr. Robson arrived and told me that you wished me to come here immediately!"

"You can thank Robson for suggesting that you were in fact exactly the Chaperon I needed to relieve me of my new responsibilities," the Duke said.

There was just an edge to his voice that told Andrina all to clearly that he was still annoyed at being saddled with them, but she thought hopefully it would not be for long.

She was quite certain that Cheryl and Sharon would quickly find husbands, and once they were married there would be no need to trouble the Duke any further.

She could not help wondering what Lady Evelyn must privately have thought of the precipitate manner in which she had been brought to Broxbourne House.

But she was left in no uncertainty about it when, after dinner was finished, the Duke bowed to his cousin and said:

"If you will excuse me, Evelyn, I will now leave and make my apologies to His Royal Highness, with whom I should have been dining."

Lady Evelyn clasped her hands together.

"Oh, Tancred, how terrible! Have we kept you from Carlton House? Surely the Regent will be angry? He hates having his parties upset!"

"There was a good excuse for it," the Duke replied, "and when I tell him that he will later have the privilege of meeting three new beauties, I am sure he will be too intrigued to be incensed with me for long."

The Duke spoke as if it was of the utmost indifference to him whether the Regent was annoyed or not, and Andrina thought it was typical of his arrogance.

"Even though I am extremely beholden to him," she told herself, "I hate him!"

But she had to admit as the Duke left them to walk across the Salon that it was difficult to imagine any man could look more distinguished or more obviously a person of consequence.

The door closed behind him and Lady Evelyn turned to Andrina.

"You brilliant, incredible child!" she cried. "How did

you do it? You must tell me before I positively die of curiosity! How did you do it?"

"Do what?" Andrina asked in surprise.

"Persuade His Grace to have you here—three of you! I cannot believe it possible!"

"But why?" Andrina asked.

"Why?" Lady Evelyn echoed. "Because if ever there was an egotistical, self-sufficient man, it is His Grace the Duke of Broxbourne! He is exactly like his father—my Uncle—who was a monster of selfishness!"

Andrina said nothing and after a moment Lady Evelyn went on:

"I immediately thought he must have fallen in love for the first time in his life; but he speaks in fact as if you were an encumbrance. If so, why is he having you here? Can you be blackmailing him, by any chance?"

Andrina could not help laughing.

"No, indeed! As it happens, I came here hoping to see the late Duke and not knowing that he had died. He was a friend of my father's when he was young."

"So Tancred told me," Lady Evelyn said. "But the last thing His Grace would want to do would be to make amends for his father's deficiencies—there were too many of them, for one thing!"

"You do not seem to be very fond of your relations," Andrina could not help saying.

Lady Evelyn gave again the light musical laugh which was characteristic of her.

"They are a moth-eaten lot—puffed up with nothing but pride! That is why it will be so exciting for me to produce a cousin like you. Are your sisters as lovely as you are?"

"They are much, much lovelier!" Andrina replied. "In fact, they are both quite beautiful . . . incredibly beautiful!"

She drew in her breath and then said bravely:

"Please help them, Lady Evelyn. This is the one chance they will ever have of meeting the right people and finding husbands."

"So that is why you have come to London!" Lady Evelyn exclaimed. "I guessed it!"

"When you see Cheryl and Sharon, I'm sure you will understand," Andrina said. "We have been living a very dull existence in Cheshire and there is nobody near us who would make a suitable husband for either of them."

"You have given me just the sort of task I enjoy!" Lady Evelyn smiled. "The first thing you and I must do tomorrow is to go shopping. I can see that you need clothes, and so do I! As for your sisters, no-one must have so much as a glimpse of them until they are properly gowned."

"Will that take long?" Andrina asked.

"We have to make sure that they are equipped in the very latest fashion as soon as they set foot in London," Lady Evelyn replied. "Besides, I have planned that the Ball shall take place at the end of the week!"

"So quickly?" Andrina exclaimed.

"The quicker the better!" Lady Evelyn said. "It is important that you should be invited to all the other Balls, Masques, riots, and assemblies that are being given this Season. The moment it is learnt that a Ball is to take place in Broxbourne House, we shall be besieged by every hostess of any importance."

Lady Evelyn's words were prophetic, and long before the Ball Andrina found herself being carried away on a flood-tide of excitement, expenditure, and speculation which made her feel as if she must lose her identity.

The first morning they had left Broxbourne House immediately after breakfast, and taking the Duke's carriage to Bond Street they went first to the shop of Madame Bertin, who, Lady Evelyn informed Andrina, was the smartest dress-maker in London.

Madame Bertin, after taking one look at the gown Andrina was wearing, was at first somewhat supercilious—until she learnt who Lady Evelyn was and understood that she was to dress three young ladies who were the wards of His Grace the Duke of Broxbourne.

From that moment she was all ingratiating smiles and

brought from the work-room unfinished gowns that had in fact been ordered by other clients, promising that some of them would be completed by the following day, if they were definitely ordered.

Andrina was so bewildered at the beauty and the smartness of the garments, each of which seemed more alluring than the last, that she would have accepted anything that Madame Bertin suggested.

But Lady Evelyn was far more choosy and Andrina was very grateful to her for her discrimination and good taste.

Fortunately she knew the exact measurements of both Cheryl and Sharon, having made gowns for them for the last five years.

"As débutantes they must wear white," Lady Evelyn said firmly.

"Cheryl looks lovely in white," Andrina said, "but Sharon is dark with a magnolia skin and looks her best in colours."

"No débutante should wear anything but white," Lady Evelyn insisted.

But the problem was solved by Madame Bertin, who suggested that one of Sharon's evening-gowns should be of silver net over white. While on another gown there was lace heavily embroidered with gold, which encircled the décolletage and made three frills round the hem of the skirt.

It was difficult to imagine that any gowns could be so light, so ethereal, and indeed so transparent, Andrina thought.

Gossamer net, gauzes, tulles, jaconet muslins, and sarsnets were all utilised, and whether they were embroidered, embellished, or run through with strands of silver and gold, they still revealed every curve and contour of the wearer's body.

Sharon had indeed been right in what she had said about the "clothes offering glimpses of breasts and legs to ardent young men"!

But Andrina was prepared to trust Lady Evelyn and

actually when the gowns were on they were not as pro-
vocative as they had appeared in the hand.

By the time they returned to Broxbourne House for
luncheon it seemed to Andrina that they had bought
mountains of clothes, and she could not help wondering
a little apprehensively if they had spent too much of the
precious five hundred pounds which she hoped the
Duke would get from the sale of her mother's necklace.

But Lady Evelyn had not finished.

There were bonnets, shoes, stockings, night-gowns,
gloves, sun-shades, and a dozen other things to be
bought during the afternoon. Hand-bags or reticules
were now in vogue because in the clinging muslins
pockets could no longer be hidden.

Andrina let herself be swept along on the tide without protest.

It was only when they were back again at
Broxbourne House and Lady Evelyn had gone upstairs
to lie down that she thought she had better speak to the
Duke and find out if in fact they had overspent.

She followed Lady Evelyn upstairs to the bed-rooms,
but instead of resting, as Her Ladyship had suggested,
she went down again to ask the Butler if the Duke was
in the house.

"He is in the Library, Miss."

"Then would you ask His Grace if I may speak to
him?" Andrina enquired.

"I will announce you, Miss. His Grace is alone."

Andrina followed him to the room where the previous day she had found the Duke when she had expected to meet his father.

She was conscious that she now looked very different
from the girl who had arrived wearing a gown she had
altered herself and which she now knew was, in
Madame Bertin's eyes, only fit for the bonfire.

Because she was so slim, she had been able to fit into
one of Madame Bertin's models which she kept to show
her clients.

Of hyacinth-blue, it was cut in the new line with a
very high waist, small puffed sleeves, and yet much

more ornamented than the gowns had been during the War when trimmings which must come from Lyons and other parts of France were impossible to obtain.

Lady Evelyn had already instructed the maid who looked after Andrina to arrange her hair in a different style, and she was conscious that she looked her best.

It gave her some confidence as the Butler opened the Library door and announced, as he had done before:

"Miss Maldon, Your Grace!"

The Duke was sitting in an arm-chair reading *The Times*.

He looked up as Andrina entered, and she thought that he deliberately stared at her for a few seconds before he rose to his feet.

She reached his side, trying to walk proudly, holding her chin high, conscious of the effect he invariably had of making her feel shy and overwhelmed by his commanding and assertive manner.

"You wish to see me?" he asked, his eyes on her face.

"I know Your Grace has no desire to be worried by details," Andrina said a little breathlessly, "but I thought I ought to tell you that Her Ladyship and I have spent a great deal of money today. I am sure it will not come to more than you will obtain for the necklace. At the same time, there will be other expenses, and I would not wish to be in Your Grace's debt."

"That would worry you?" the Duke asked.

"As I have already said," Andrina replied with dignity, "we must not be a burden on you financially, and you must tell me when I can spend no more."

The Duke did not speak, and after a moment she said:

"I do not know quite what to say to Lady Evelyn about her own gowns. She informed the dress-maker and the other shops that all the bills were to be sent to you! But I will pay for Lady Evelyn's purchases as well as for our own."

"Is not that rather profligate?" the Duke enquired in a tone which made her think he was sneering at her.

"Even five hundred pounds, if that is what your necklace fetches, will not last forever!"

"It should last for two months," Andrina said, "and of course we would wish to pay for the Ball—the champagne and the Band."

"I think I should make this clear," the Duke answered. "Whatever hospitality I offer my guests in my own house is my responsibility."

"If it were not for us, you would not have had to entertain them at all," Andrina argued.

"I am not in the habit of accepting money from women."

"There is no need to talk like that," Andrina said sharply. "You make it sound as if I should not have suggested it; but you know as well as I do that you did not wish us to come here. I should not want to feel that we are battening on your good nature, and certainly not financially!"

"If you do not like the way I run things in my house," the Duke replied, "the alternative is very obvious."

He is being deliberately aggressive, Andrina thought.

"I cannot understand why you will not see sense," she protested. "I forced myself and my sisters upon you . . . I admit that . . . but we do not wish to be the kind of impecunious relations who are out to get everything they can. I realise they exist in every family, but I see no reason why we should put ourselves in that position unnecessarily."

"You got your own way in one regard," the Duke replied, "but I am damned if I am going to be bullied in any other. I make my arrangements as they suit me, and all you have to do is accede to them!"

He spoke sharply and Andrina felt herself flush, not with embarrassment but with anger.

"Very well, Your Grace," she said, "and of course I am . . . humbly and servilely grateful!"

She spoke ironically, curtseyed and went from the room, afraid that she might say something which she would later regret.

'Why must he be so pig-headed?' she thought, then wondered if perhaps she was being absurd to split straws.

He was doing so much for them already, and it would not possibly matter to him who paid for the champagne and the Band. He was rich enough not to notice it.

At the same time, Andrina felt almost as if she were sinking in shifting sand, and sooner or later it would close over her head and suffocate her.

When Cheryl and Sharon arrived, it was Sharon who told her that she was being absurd to worry about anything except the fact that they were in London and making their début in the most auspicious circumstances.

"The Wards of a Duke! A Ball! Ah, Andrina, how did you manage it?" she asked, and flung her arms round her older sister's neck.

"To tell you the truth," Andrina answered, "I never thought he would agree. But of course, we are paying for ourselves. I gave him Mama's necklace and told him that that would cover our expenses. But he will not let me pay for the Ball."

"Why should he?" Sharon asked. "After all, it is taking place in his house. It is very kind of him to give it."

"I would feel much happier," Andrina said, "if we were responsible for the champagne and the Band, which, of course, would mean that we would have fewer gowns."

"Do not be silly!" Sharon replied. "If we do get married, we shall want every penny that is left to buy our trousseaux. Have you thought of that?"

"I suppose I have not really taken it into account," Andrina admitted.

"Well, for goodness' sake, Andrina, let him give us anything he wishes," Sharon begged. "I gather he has never done anything like this before."

"Who told you that?" Andrina asked.

"Lady Davenport. She was absolutely astonished that we should be coming to London to stay at Broxbourne

House. The Duke told her in his letter that Lady Evelyn was to be our Chaperon, but she still seemed to think it reprehensible that we should be guests in the house of a bachelor."

"I do not think it is because he is a bachelor," Andrina said, "but because he is a Duke and a very autocratic one!"

It was Cheryl, who was always more sensitive to other people's feelings than Sharon, who exclaimed:

"You sound as if you do not like him, Andrina."

"To be honest," Andrina replied, "I think he is far too pleased with himself, besides being a tyrant and a despot!"

She spoke so violently that both Cheryl and Sharon looked at her in consternation.

"Why should you feel like that?" Sharon asked after a moment.

Cheryl looked worried and took one of Andrina's hands in hers.

"If it upsets you, Andrina," she said in her soft voice, "we can go back home and not worry about making our début in London. Hugo said I would not like it here."

"Hugo is talking a lot of nonsense!" Andrina said. "But the Duke is a difficult man, and of course we have to be very careful not to upset him."

"It is very, very kind of him to have us," Cheryl said.

"When are we going to meet him?" Sharon asked.

As if her words were a cue, Andrina thought to herself, for the entrance of the Demon King, there was a knock at the door.

They were all in Andrina's room and three heads turned simultaneously.

"Come in!" she said.

It was one of the maids, bringing a message to say that the Duke wished to see the young ladies in the Salon.

Andrina gave a little cry.

"Change! Change your clothes quickly!" she said. "I do not wish him to see you in your travelling-clothes, but in the new gowns I have bought for you."

She glanced at the clock.

"We can keep him waiting for five minutes, but not a second longer!"

The girls hurried to their bed-rooms, which adjoined Andrina's. She followed Cheryl to help her into an afternoon-gown made of white lace slotted through with blue ribbon and with a sash of the same colour.

She chose the blue which was the same colour as Cheryl's eyes, and when she had quickly arranged her hair and added two bows to hold her curls in place she looked so lovely that Andrina thought it would be impossible for any man to resist her.

Sharon's gown was also white, but cut in a more classical shape and trimmed with touches of leaf-green which made her skin seem more than ever like a magnolia.

She looked exotic and very beautiful as five minutes later she followed Andrina and Cheryl downstairs and they entered the Salon to find the Duke at the far end of it.

They advanced towards him and all three girls curtseyed almost simultaneously.

"Your Grace, may I present my sisters?" Andrina asked, and she could not keep the triumph out of her voice.

"This is Cheryl . . . and this is Sharon!"

The sisters curtseyed again. Then Sharon said impulsively:

"This is the most exciting thing that has ever happened to us! And you look exactly as a Duke should look!"

"And how is that?" the Duke asked.

"Very grand and very impressive!" Sharon answered. "I should like to see you wearing your coronet!"

"Perhaps you will have that privilege on another occasion," the Duke replied with a twist of his lips.

Andrina knew that he was being sarcastic.

At the same time, she had been watching closely when she effected the introduction, and she had not missed the expression of surprise in his eyes when he looked at Cheryl, then at Sharon.

'He did not really believe that they could be as beautiful as I had told him!' Andrina thought to herself.

"This is a very big house!" Cheryl said after a moment, and there was a tremor in her voice which told Andrina that she was nervous.

She took her sister by the hand and drew her to the window.

"There is the garden," she said. "Look how beautifully it is kept, and the flowers are exquisite! His Grace is having it lit with fairy-lights on the night of the Ball. It will be very romantic!"

Cheryl's fingers were cold in hers, but Sharon was talking excitedly to the Duke and after a moment he said to Andrina:

"I do not know whether Lady Evelyn has told you, but we have been asked to dine with the Duchess of Devonshire. It is only a dinner-party, but I expect the young people will dance afterwards."

"Thank goodness we have some new gowns!" Sharon exclaimed. "I have read about Devonshire House in a magazine. It is very impressive, and the Duchess is said to be very beautiful!"

"I can see you are well informed!" the Duke said. "We will leave here at half past seven. Lady Evelyn insists that I accompany you, otherwise she says that no-one will believe I am acting as your Guardian."

He walked from the room as he spoke and Andrina followed him with her eyes.

She was certain that he was finding it irksome to be forced by his cousin into accompanying them this evening, but she was sure that Lady Evelyn was right and the Social world would find it hard to credit that the rumours already circulating in London were not just a practical joke.

"I do not think he wants to go to the party," Cheryl said, and her expression was troubled.

"He always talks like that," Andrina said soothingly. "You must not pay any attention to him, Cheryl."

"I think he is rather fascinating!" Sharon said. "I expect the reason he has never married is that he has been crossed in love!"

Andrina could not help wondering if that was in fact true.

Could that be the explanation of the Duke's cynicism? And perhaps too why he liked to be self-sufficient and a bachelor?

But she had no more time to think about the Duke.

For the moment she was concerned only to keep Cheryl happy and from being intimidated by the largeness of the house, the enormous number of servants there were to wait on them, and by Lady Evelyn.

Not that there was any reason for her to be afraid of Lady Evelyn, who was so delighted herself at the thought of going to a party that she appeared to be laughing about everything as well as helping the girls to look their best.

The hair-dresser had been ordered to come to their rooms and attend to one after the other.

There was a great deal of discussion as to which of the many gowns that had already arrived they should wear for their first appearance.

Then finally, when first Cheryl and then Sharon was dressed, Andrina realised that she had only a little time to dress herself, and took the first gown that came to hand.

Because the girls were to wear white for their first Season and she was no longer a débutante, the dresses she had chosen for herself—and there were not nearly as many as had been bought for Cheryl and Sharon— were in the pale colours that her mother had always wanted her to wear.

"You will never go wrong if you follow the flowers, darling," she had said. "Their colours are never harsh or discordant, and even when a flower is crimson it has soft tints and shades about it which are never harsh or crude."

The gown that Andrina wore tonight was another blue, this time the blue of the forget-me-not.

It was rather simpler and without the frills that trimmed Cheryl's gown or the embroidered lace on Sharon's.

Andrina hoped too that it was cheaper, but she was quite certain that Madame Bertin was exorbitantly expensive for whatever she made, and she was determined as soon as she had time to find a cheaper shop where they could procure any other gowns they required.

When finally they were ready to go downstairs, Lady Evelyn came to collect them, looking magnificent in a gown of deep purple and wearing on her shoulders a spray of purple orchids.

"How lovely those orchids are!" Andrina exclaimed.

To her surprise, Lady Evelyn looked a little embarrassed.

"I always wore flowers when I was in Brussels," she said, "so I thought that just for tonight I would be a little extravagant."

"They are very becoming, Ma'am," Andrina said dutifully.

But she could not help wondering if Lady Evelyn expected her to pay for them!

Then she told herself that it was the least they could do and perhaps a simple way of expressing their gratitude.

Andrina had been right in thinking that the Social world would quickly recognise the beauty of Cheryl and Sharon.

From the moment they appeared at the Devonshire House party there was no doubt as to their success.

Andrina listened proudly to the flattering remarks that were made to her about Cheryl and Sharon, and although she was often included in the almost overwhelming flattery she told herself that it was just politeness, and that she was of little importance beside her younger sisters.

And yet she found that people were far more interesting to talk to than she had expected.

That first evening she sat at dinner next to the Duke

of Wellington. She was thrilled, as she had always longed to meet the man she had admired all her life.

He was extremely pleasant and she was not to know that the Duke had always had an eye for a pretty woman and was well-known for his amatory affairs even though he was discreet about them.

She told him how her father had spoken of the Battle of Assaye and how brilliant the Duke had been in command.

"What brought me through many difficulties in the Mahretta War and in the negotiation for peace was the British good faith and nothing else," the Duke told her.

Andrina noticed his flashing eyes and remembered that, after Waterloo, she had read that Sir Alexander Frazer had said:

"Cold and indifferent . . . in the beginning of battle, when the moment of difficulty comes, intelligence flashes from the eyes of this wonderful man; and he rises superior to all that can be imagined."

On the other side of her she found herself neglecting the Earl of Crowhurst, which was inevitable, in comparison with the Hero of Waterloo.

He was not attractive, in fact Andrina thought he was ugly and there was something debauched about the deep lines under his heavy-lidded eyes and the fullness of his sensual lips.

As she was so busy talking to the Duke she did not have any conversation with him until the dinner was well advanced, and when at last, remembering her manners, she turned to the Earl, he said:

"You have been ignoring me, Miss Maldon, and I am extremely piqued about it!"

"Please forgive me if I have seemed rude," Andrina pleaded, "but I was so excited to meet the Duke of Wellington. My father has talked of him ever since I was a child, and I have read about every battle in which he has ever taken part."

"I have fought on different battle-fields," the Earl remarked, "but in my way I have been equally successful!"

"On what battle-fields has that been?" Andrina enquired.

"That of love!" he replied.

He saw the surprised look in her eyes and added:

"You are very beautiful, Miss Maldon, as I am sure an army of men have already told you!"

"On the contrary, My Lord," Andrina replied, "I have only just arrived in London; in the country people are not so outspoken."

"Is it true the noble Duke is setting up a Nursery in Broxbourne House?"

"If you are referring to the fact that he is introducing my sisters and me to Society," Andrina answered coldly, "then it is!"

The Earl looked across the table at Cheryl, then at Sharon.

"I must compliment Broxbourne on his excellent taste! Where could he have found three such exquisite creatures?"

Andrina felt this was dangerous ground and said quickly:

"We are relatives of the Duke, but will you not tell me about yourself, My Lord?"

"As long as I may talk about myself and you, that is all I ask," the Earl of Crowhurst said softly, "and I want to talk about you, lovely lady!"

There was a caress in his voice which made Andrina look at him a little apprehensively.

Then she told herself that he was only like one of those tiresome old men who used to flirt with her when they called on her father.

"Are you interested in horses, My Lord?" she asked, hoping she would divert his attention.

"I am interested only in the prettiest little filly I have seen for many years!" he answered. "And I have just learnt that her name is Andrina!"

He went on paying her compliments and talking in a low, intimate voice which made her feel embarrassed; so that in the end she was glad when dinner was finished and the Duchess took the ladies from the room.

After dinner there was dancing and Andrina expected that the Earl would think himself too old to take the floor with the Duchess's relatives—the young Cavendishes and girls who were mostly Cheryl and Sharon's age.

But he came up to Andrina as soon as the gentlemen had left the Dining-Room, and although at first she refused he finally persuaded her to dance a waltz which had been introduced to London after the Peace.

Fortunately the girls, who all enjoyed dancing, had learnt the quadrilles, which Sharon informed them were all the rage, and also the steps of the new Viennese Waltz.

The Belle Assemblée had reported that a high-brow party met daily at Devonshire House to learn dancing all over again.

"I want to put my arm round you," the Earl said. "Your figure is exquisite! I really think someone should sculpt you as Venus."

Andrina, unsophisticated though she might be, was quite aware of what he insinuated, and she stiffened in his arms and decided that she had taken a dislike to the Earl of Crowhurst.

When they left Devonshire House the Duke did not accompany them, and they were alone in the carriage with Lady Evelyn when she exclaimed:

"What an evening! You have all been a huge success! Cheryl, I could see that the Marquis of Glen was delighted with you, and Andrina has certainly made a conquest of the Earl of Crowhurst!"

"I hope not!" Andrina said quickly. "I think he is a horrible man!"

"My dear child, he is a great catch!" Lady Evelyn said.

"He has never been married?" Sharon asked.

"Twice, as it happens," Lady Evelyn replied. "His first wife died a year after they married when he was very young, and his second wife had a bad fall out hunting three years ago. They tried to save her life, but had they succeeded she would have been a helpless cripple, so it was in fact far better that she should die."

"That was very sad for her husband," Cheryl said, who was always touched by any tale of suffering or unhappiness.

"He soon consoled himself," Lady Evelyn remarked drily. "At the same time, if he should be serious where you are concerned, Andrina, it would be a great feather in your cap! He is extremely wealthy and his Estate in Hampshire is, I believe, magnificent!"

"I am not interested in the Earl," Andrina said coldly, "nor, for that matter, in anyone else. It is Cheryl and Sharon who must find nice husbands."

"Well, the Marquis of Glen is certainly nice," Lady Evelyn remarked. "He is the oldest son of the Duke of Arkrae and is of course Scottish, but none the worse for that."

Andrina drew in her breath.

How wonderful it would be if the Marquis should fall in love with Cheryl and she would eventually become a Duchess. It was what she had always longed for her to be.

She had noticed the Marquis, a sandy-haired young man, dancing with Cheryl and had thought him rather insignificant. But he appeared quiet and polite and he would not, she thought with satisfaction, frighten Cheryl as someone like the Earl would do.

Cheryl was, she knew, already frightened of the Duke. He was the type of man she did not understand and Andrina had made up her mind to keep her away from him as much as possible.

Sharon was different. She was never in awe of anyone, and as she had already said, she found the Duke fascinating.

At the Devonshire's party she seemed always to have two or three men standing round her, laughing at what she said.

Adrina had never doubted that wherever Sharon went she would be a success.

Then the thought came to her that perhaps Sharon might marry the Duke.

If Cheryl was to be the Duchess of Arkrae, why should Sharon not be the Duchess of Broxbourne?

It was certainly an idea, and she wondered whether the Duke preferred fair or dark-haired women. If the former, it might be very difficult to persuade Cheryl to consider him as a husband.

Andrina's thoughts about marriage for her sisters kept her awake long after she had gone to bed.

The girls were tired after their long drive but, despite all that she and Lady Evelyn had done during the day and the excitement of dining at the Devonshire House, Andrina found it impossible to sleep.

Finally she rose from her bed and walked to the window.

Her room looked out over the front of the house, and as she drew back the curtains she saw a carriage coming up the short drive and turning beneath her under the pillared portico.

It was the Duke returning home and she wondered where he had been. It must be three hours since they had left Devonshire House.

Had he been to his Club? Or had he perhaps visited some lady who had been waiting for him when he was no longer socially engaged?

Andrina knew, because she had listened to her father talking about it, that gentlemen were interested in actresses, in the singers at Vauxhall Gardens, and in "ladies" who might be very beautiful but were not accepted by any Social hostess.

Was that the sort of woman, Andrina wondered, that the Duke had been to see at this hour of the night?

She told herself it was very probable. After all, that was the sort of woman he had thought she was when he had kissed her in the Parlour of the Inn.

She felt herself once again growing angry at the thought.

Then she remembered the strange feeling his kiss

had evoked in her, a sensation like forked-lightning running through her body, a pain, then a pleasure that was indescribable.

"How dare he?" Andrina asked herself aloud, and abruptly pulled the curtains together again.

CHAPTER FOUR

Andrina looked round the Ball-Room with a feeling of triumph.

Nothing could have been more impressive or magnificent than the Ball-Room at Broxbourne House, decorated with garlands of white flowers and with the long French windows opening onto the garden which glittered with fairy-lights.

The Band was wearing a uniform of red with gold braid, and the dancers were a spectacle in themselves, from the glittering jewels of the ladies to the flashing decorations of the gentlemen.

The Prince Regent had honoured the Duke by dining at Broxbourne House, and they had sat down forty to dinner. Afterwards two hundred guests had arrived, all of them, Andrina knew, among the most important and distinguished people in London.

Watching the dancers, she thought that Cheryl had exceeded all her hopes and expectations.

Her gown of white gauze, decorated with tiny rows of lace caught up with small bunches of snow-drops, was the ideal frame for a débutante. And who, she asked herself, could be more beautiful than Cheryl when she was laughing and happy?

Her golden hair glinted beneath the thousands of candles in the huge crystal chandeliers and her blue eyes, turned upwards to look at her partner, the Marquis of Glen, were sparkling.

Everything, Andrina told herself, was almost too good to be true.

She thought the Marquis a somewhat ineffective man, and he was certainly not good-looking compared with the Duke or with many of the other resplendent and handsome gentlemen in the room.

But Cheryl liked him and was obviously not nervous or shy when she was with him, and that was the first step in the right direction to her becoming a Duchess.

There was a satisfied smile on Andrina's lips as she looked round for Sharon, to be replaced by a faint frown between her eyes.

Sharon, in a gown of silver lace over a petticoat of silver lamé, looked exotic and exciting. Only the slimness of her figure and the look in her eyes revealed to those who were perceptive how young and innocent she was in reality.

In her dark hair she wore two diamond stars which glittered in the candle-light.

Andrina's only decoration was a wreath of pink roses which matched her dress.

To look different from her sisters, her gown was of rose-pink gauze over a pale satin, decorated only with small bunches of roses and velvet ribbons.

A number of gentlemen, with a lamentable lack of originality, had told her she looked like a rose, and she knew without conceit that the gown was very becoming.

But Andrina had in fact hurried over her own *toilette* when dressing for the Ball and she was supervising Cheryl's when there was a knock at the door and without waiting for an answer Lady Evelyn joined them.

"Can you imagine it possible, girls?" she asked. "I have just received a message from His Grace to say that we can wear any of the family jewels which take our fancy!"

"The family jewels?" Andrina repeated, and at that moment Sharon came in from an adjoining room.

"That is just what I was thinking we lacked!" she exclaimed, having overheard what Lady Evelyn had said. "We are all very elegant but we need the extra touch that only gems can give to make us really smart!"

"That is exactly what I thought myself," Lady Evelyn said. "At my age jewels are as important to a woman as the cosmetics with which she embellishes her complexion."

"Where are they?" Sharon asked.

"I will show you," Lady Evelyn answered with a smile.

They all went downstairs to Mr. Robson's office to find him waiting for them, having already received his instructions from the Duke.

He opened a heavy iron door that was situated in a corner of the room and they saw what Andrina privately thought of as an Aladdin's cave.

There were shelves on which reposed leather-, velvet-, and satin-covered boxes, and when each one was opened by Mr. Robson the jewellery they contained made them all gasp in astonishment.

There was a set of sapphires and diamonds which comprised an enormous tiara, a necklace, bracelets, brooches, and rings, and there were other sets equally magnificent in emeralds, rubies, diamonds, and pearls.

There were other pieces of jewellery, many of them historical, which had been brought into the family either through marriage or by being acquired by the various Dukes on their journeys abroad.

Sharon went into ecstasies over each new jewel she was shown and even Cheryl seemed a little excited by them.

"What shall we choose?" Sharon cried.

"I should have liked to wear the sapphires," Lady Evelyn said, "but alas, they will not go with my gown. I always thought they were the finest gems in the Broxbourne collection and I remember His Grace's mother looking absolutely magnificent in them!"

She turned to the Secretary.

"Is that not so, Mr. Robson?"

"Her Grace was one of the most beautiful women I have ever seen," he answered.

"Will the Duke mind their being worn by anyone else?" Andrina asked.

She was really speaking to Mr. Robson, but Lady Evelyn heard and said:

"I see no reason why he should mind. His mother died when he was six and it is unlikely that he directly remembers her."

Andrina said nothing but she felt quite sure that the Duke did remember his mother. After all, she could remember hers long before she was six, and her father too in the years when he had been young and gay and always good-tempered.

"I will wear the diamonds," Lady Evelyn said with a last wistful look at the sapphires. "Now, girls, what is your choice?"

"I think all Cheryl will need is a small string of pearls," Andrina said firmly. "I am sure it would be incorrect for a débutante to wear much jewellery."

Lady Evelyn gave her a little smile.

"You are quite right, Andrina," she said. "I should have said that, not you. It would be ostentatious and in bad taste. A string of pearls would be perfect for Cheryl."

"Why not these, Miss Sharon?" Mr. Robson suggested.

"I want something that glitters," Sharon said firmly.

He opened another box and inside they saw two brooches shaped like stars and glittering with blue-white diamonds.

Andrina fixed them in Sharon's hair and they certainly much enhanced her appearance and were in perfect harmony with the glittering silver of her gown.

"And what about you, Andrina?" Lady Evelyn asked.

Andrina shook her head.

"I have no need for jewellery," she said. "There is a wreath which goes with my gown and that is all I require."

She spoke so firmly that nobody argued. Then, having thanked Mr. Robson, they returned upstairs.

"Why did you not choose a pretty bracelet?" Cheryl asked when they had reached the bed-rooms.

"It would only be hidden by my gloves," Andrina said quickly.

She could not explain to Cheryl or to anyone else why she felt a reluctance to accept the Duke's offer of appearing in the Broxbourne jewels.

She somehow felt it was too incongruous to wear something that was so closely connected with him personally when she knew that she disliked him and that he, as he had said himself, had embroiled himself in their "crazy, senseless scheme" against his better judgment!

It was different where Cheryl and Sharon were concerned.

She was the one who had forced the Duke into agreeing to introduce them to the Social world, and in consequence she would not accept from him anything that was not entirely necessary.

Looking at Sharon now, Andrina realised that she was dancing for the second time that evening with a tall and handsome Russian whom they had met at Almack's.

It was Sharon who had been almost too excited to speak when on Wednesday night Lady Evelyn had told them they were to visit Almack's.

The temple of the *Beau Monde*, about which she had read in her magazines and which was the most exclusive, most select place in London, was to open its doors to them and they were on the List!

It was, Andrina had thought at first sight, disappointing after so much had been said and written about it.

A suite of Assembly Rooms in King Street, St. James's, it seemed a quite ordinary place of entertainment, with refreshments consisting of lemonade and tea, bread and butter and stale cake, until one looked at those who were being entertained.

Lady Evelyn of course knew everyone and she had

already told her charges on the way to Almack's how fortunate they were to have received their vouchers from Lady Cowper within a few days of arriving in London.

"The Foot-Guards boast of three hundred Officers," Lady Evelyn said, "but of those only six are admitted to the Club."

"Do the gentlemen gamble?" Sharon asked. She had been reading about some of the other Clubs in London.

"It was suggested a short while ago," Lady Evelyn replied, "but the Patronesses said that if card-tables were introduced, the girls would lose all their partners. Men would always rather play than dance!"

She laughed.

"No, you are the entertainment tonight, and make sure that you do not miss this opportunity."

It would be difficult for most girls, Andrina thought later, to be noticed when the Patronesses of Almack's were themselves so beautiful.

Lady Cowper, who greeted them, was at twenty-nine at the height of perfection. She had an almost classic profile, large expressive eyes, and a head that was set proudly on graceful shoulders.

Andrina was to learn later that Lady Cowper was much the sweetest and kindest of all the Patronesses, but she could understand too why Lady Jersey, who was known as "Silence" amongst her friends because she never stopped talking, was fascinating.

Lady Sefton, another Patroness, was amiable, and the Princess de Lieven, the wife of the Russian Ambassador, had a personality it was impossible for anyone to ignore.

She had an infinite capacity for making mischief, and power was an obsession with her.

She entertained all the important men in London in her husband's Embassy in Ashburham Street and she believed she could sway in Russia's favour the opinions of men like the Duke of Wellington, Lord Castlereagh, and Lord Palmerston.

Yet she was not clever enough to realise that they saw through her.

In fact Lady Evelyn told Andrina that the Duke of Wellington had said that the Princess was "a *femme d'esprit* who can and will betray everyone in turn if it should suit her purpose."

It had been the Princess who had presented Count Ivan Birkendorff to Sharon, and when he had taken her onto the dance-floor a great number of those present had turned to look at two such handsome and attractive young people waltzing together.

The Princess de Lieven had introduced at Almack's the waltz, which was considered at first to be extremely immoral.

"Even Lord Byron was shocked by it!" Lady Evelyn told Andrina, "and he only permitted Lady Caroline Lamb to waltz after he had grown tired of her!"

Although Lord Byron had gone to Italy the previous year, the scandal he had caused with Caroline Lamb was still the *en dit*, Andrina found, by the ladies who called on Lady Evelyn. But at the moment she was concerned only that there should be no gossip about Cheryl and Sharon.

She was also very anxious that Sharon should not waste her beauty, her wit, and her fascinations on ineligible young men.

"After all," she told herself with a little sigh, "we have so little time."

Two months ... only two months in which to find Cheryl and Sharon husbands! And if they failed there was only an ignominious return to Bigger Stukeby and the loneliness and boredom of the Manor House.

It was something she hardly dared to contemplate, and yet always at the back of her mind there was the spectre of failure.

Every tick of the clock brought them nearer to the moment when their money would have run out and they could no longer impose on the Duke's hospitality.

Andrina had made it her business to find out all she could about Count Ivan Birkendorff.

She learnt that he came from a distinguished Russian family, but he was not at all rich and was only a very junior Diplomat. It was expected by the gossips that with his good looks and undeniable charm, he would marry into the British aristocracy and chose a bride with money.

Andrina had related this to Sharon, and yet here at the Ball she was dancing with the Count again and looking exceedingly lovely as she did so.

"How can she be so foolish tonight of all nights," Andrina asked herself, "when every Nobleman of importance is here?"

Could any girls have been more lucky than to have a Ball given for them which was graced by the Prince Regent and for which every important hostess in London had given a dinner-party?

Andrina was determined to speak to Sharon, and as her sister waltzing round the room came near her she stepped forward.

The Count saw her and stopped dancing but his arms still encircled his partner's waist.

"Your skirt is caught up a little," Andrina said. Then as she pretended to adjust it and Sharon turned her head to see what was wrong, she said in a whisper:

"Dance with the Duke. If he does not ask you, you must ask him!"

She did not wait for her sister's reply, but stood back as if she had completed her task and smiled at the Count.

"I hope you are enjoying the Ball!" she said.

"How could I be anything but rapturously happy at the moment?" he replied.

He bowed, but when he would have resumed the waltz the Band stopped playing.

"You dance divinely!" Andrina heard him say to Sharon. "When will you honour me again?"

Andrina had the feeling that Sharon was going to give him another dance and, putting her hand on her sister's arm, she said:

"I think, dearest, we must find Lady Evelyn."

She thought that Sharon was about to refuse, when at that very moment a voice at her elbow said:

"I have been told by Lady Evelyn to discover if you both have plenty of partners?"

It was the Duke, and Andrina replied:

"We have indeed, Your Grace, but of course we are still waiting for our host to lead us onto the floor, as is, I believe, correct."

"I am afraid my etiquette in such matters is limited," the Duke replied, "but of course if you . . ."

Andrina, realising that he was about to invite her to be his partner, quickly drew Sharon forward.

"Sharon has been hoping all the evening that Your Grace would dance with her," she said. "Is that not so, dearest?"

Her fingers pressed her sister's arm as she spoke and obediently Sharon replied:

"I should be very disappointed if you did not consider me important enough, Your Grace."

"I think, as we are talking about matters of protocol," the Duke replied with a hint of laughter in his voice which told Andrina quite clearly that he had realised what she was doing, "I should take my protégées in order, starting with the eldest."

Andrina, looking at him, saw a cynical twist to his lips and guessed that he knew that the last thing she wanted was to dance with him.

"It is an honour, Your Grace," she said, "but unfortunately I am already promised for this dance."

She looked round hastily as she spoke, seeking a familiar face amongst the men standing talking with each other or escorting their partners back to the Chaperons.

She could not immediately recognise anyone. Then a voice she most disliked said:

"I think, fair charmer, you are promised to me!"

Andrina gave a start and saw that standing behind her was the man she had taken a dislike to at the first dinner-party they had attended—Lord Crowhurst.

She had in fact seen him in the distance at Almack's,

but he had been with Lady Castlereagh and the Princess Esterhazy and although he had bowed he had not sought her company nor asked her for a dance.

He had obviously overheard what she said to the Duke and it was impossible to refuse him without being rude. Besides, it meant that in the circumstances the Duke would be obliged to partner Sharon.

"I think you must be right, My Lord," she said. "I am afraid I have muddled my partners into such a tangle that it is beyond unravelling."

"Do not let us trouble our heads about anyone else but ourselves," Lord Crowhurst answered.

The Band started up and without looking again at the Duke, Andrina allowed Lord Crowhurst to lead her onto the dance-floor.

He danced well, which surprised her. At the same time, she knew that she disliked him and there was something within her which was revolted by the touch of his hand, even though she was wearing gloves.

Fortunately the dance was not a waltz, where they would have been closer, but a quadrille, so that it was impossible to have an intimate conversation.

When the dance was over Lord Crowhurst put his hand under Andrina's elbow and moved her skilfully through one of the open French windows and into the garden outside.

She hardly realised where he was leading her because, as she had tried to do during the dance, she was still looking to see whether Sharon was dancing with the Duke.

The room had been so crowded that she had not been able to observe them, though she thought that she saw Cheryl's white gown disappearing down one of the lighted paths.

Because she thought it was somewhat indiscreet for Cheryl to leave the Ball-Room with the Marquis and it might incur the censure of the more stiff-necked Dowagers, she hurried after the white gown.

It was only when with the Earl beside her she had reached almost the centre of the garden that she real-

ised that the girl in front who had stopped with her
partner to look at a small fountain was not Cheryl. She
merely wore a white dress which in some way
resembled that of her sister.

Andrina gave a audible sigh of relief and realised
that she and the Earl had walked quickly but had in
fact said nothing to each other.

She turned for the first time to look at him, and she
could see him quite clearly in the light of the Chinese
lanterns which hung from the branches of the trees.

He seemed to her to be more unpleasant-looking
than she remembered, with his deep-set eyes and dark
lines of debauchery beneath them and his thick, sensual lips.

"Do you always Chaperon your sisters with such
ardour?" the Earl enquired.

Andrina felt confused.

She had not thought he would realise that she had
been pursuing the girl in the white gown.

"Cheryl and Sharon are very young," she replied.
"They have never been in London before. Because
they are so lovely I have to look after them."

"And who looks after you?" the Earl enquired.

There was something caressing in the way he said
the last word and Andrina replied lightly:

"I assure you, My Lord, I can look after myself!"

"I am glad to hear that," he replied. "Come, I have
something to say to you."

He took her hand as he spoke and led her down a
little path. Without thinking, Andrina acquiesced, her
thoughts once again on Cheryl.

It was only as the path came to an end and she
found herself in a tiny arbour containing a seat on
which there were several silk cushions that she said
quickly:

"I must go back to the Ball-Room!"

"There is no hurry," the Earl replied.

"On the contrary, My Lord," Andrina contradicted,
"the next dance will have started by now and my partner will be looking for me."

"Let him look," the Earl answered. "I want to talk to you, Andrina, and here we shall not be disturbed."

She noticed the use of her Christian name and said in a reproving tone:

"This is only the second time we have met, My Lord!"

The Earl did not pretend to misunderstand her.

"That is something about which I wish to talk to you," he said. "Let us sit down."

He stood between Andrina and the path and she thought it would be undignified and rather childish to make a fuss.

She seated herself down on one of the silk cushions and said:

"This is just the sort of place that I was trying to prevent my sister Cheryl from finding!"

"As you have already told me, Cheryl is young," the Earl said, "but you can look after yourself!"

Andrina hoped he was right.

She was uncomfortably aware that he had now sat down nearer to her than was necessary. In the dim light he looked even more unpleasant and she was extremely conscious of the distaste he aroused in her.

"You are very beautiful, Andrina!" he said softly.

"I have already pointed out, My Lord, that on such short acquaintance my name is Miss Maldon, or, if you prefer, *Miss* Andrina!"

"There are many ways in which I intend to address you," the Earl replied, "and none of them starts with 'Miss'!"

Andrina felt that he had drawn even nearer and she said quickly:

"I must return. What was it you wished to say to me?"

"I wish to tell you that you are delightful, entrancing, admirable, and that I think—no, I am sure—that I have fallen in love!"

"That is ridiculous, as you well know!" Andrina said sharply. "No-one falls in love at first sight, except in a novel."

"But you must have learnt that the exception proves the rule," the Earl replied. "The moment I saw you, Andrina, I knew that we belonged to each other!"

Andrina was tense.

"I am sorry . . . My Lord . . . I can stay no longer," she said quickly. "Please forget what you have . . . said to me, because I assure you I do not take it . . . seriously!"

"Then I must convince you that I am serious," the Earl replied, "very serious, Andrina!"

As he spoke he put his arm round her waist.

Andrina instantly turned her head away from him and said in what she hoped was a cold and icy tone:

"Do not touch me, My Lord! If you do I shall scream, and that would be extremely undignified!"

"I doubt if anyone would hear you," the Earl said with a smile, "and if they did and came to your rescue, think how much gossip it would cause!"

He knew how to make things difficult, Andrina thought.

Rather than go on arguing, she tried to rise to her feet, but it was impossible with the Earl's arm round her waist, pulling her against him, and now he took her other hand in his.

"As I have already said, you are lovely, Andrina, and you excite me!"

As he spoke he bent forward and his lips were on her bare shoulder, hard against the softness of her skin.

It took her by surprise because her head was turned away from him.

Then as she felt his mouth hot and insistent it disgusted her.

She struggled but he was too strong and now he pulled her against him and his lips were on her neck.

"No . . . no!" she cried.

His kisses grew more passionate and Andrina was terrified that his mouth would possess hers.

She twisted her face away from him, but found it impossible to move her arms.

Then suddenly, driven by fear, with a super-human

effort and a strength she did not know she possessed, she fought herself free.

As the Earl clutched at her dress, she escaped him, and was running frantically down the path back towards the Ball-Room.

The dancing had started again and there were only a few people left in the garden.

Andrina's eyes were fixed on the brilliant lights coming from the uncurtained windows, until on the terrace, just before she reached the Ball-Room windows, she bumped into someone.

As she did so she realised that a man had deliberately stepped in front of her and; looking up at him, she saw that it was the Duke.

Her breath was coming quickly between her lips and for a moment it was impossible to speak.

The impact with which she had bumped into him had unsteadied her, so that he reached out to stop her from falling.

"What have you been doing," the Duke asked harshly, "or is that an unnecessary question?"

With difficulty Andrina forced herself to reply breathlessly:

"I . . . I thought I was . . . late for the . . . dance!"

"Do not lie to me!" the Duke retorted. "You have been with Crowhurst! If he has frightened you, it is everything you deserve!"

Andrina did not answer.

She was fighting for self-control and although the Duke had taken his hands from her she still felt unsteady on her feet.

She wanted to leave him, to go into the Ball-Room, but somehow was unable to move.

"Have you not enough sense, enough knowledge of proper behaviour, not to go into a garden with a man of that type?"

The Duke's voice was scathing.

"I did not . . . think," she stammered after a moment.

"You never do," he replied. "Or is it that you have

a predilection for dangerous situations, of being alone with strange men?"

"That is not . . . fair!" Andrina cried hotly, stung by the contempt in his voice and by the insinuation that she enjoyed such encounters.

"Fair?" the Duke ejaculated. "It is, if you like, crass stupidity! But it is hardly what one expects from someone of your age who pretends to be looking after her younger sisters!"

"I went into the . . . garden because I . . . thought I saw . . . Cheryl ahead of . . . me," Andrina said.

She felt that she had to explain, she had to make the Duke understand that she had not deliberately sought to be alone with the Earl in the darkness.

"It is typical that you should be fussing over your sisters instead of setting them an example by your own behaviour," the Duke snapped. "You are not such a nit-wit, Andrina, as to think that a man with Crowhurst's reputation would take you into the garden except to make love to you."

He paused to say sternly:

"If he has frightened and shocked you on this occasion, perhaps it will be a lesson that you will remember next time you go philandering!"

"How dare you . . . speak to me like . . . that!" Andrina cried, unable to repress her anger at what she thought were unjust accusations on the Duke's part.

"You forget," he said icily, "that it was you who insisted that we are related. I can hardly be expected to stand by and watch my so-called cousin deport herself in a manner which, to say the least of it, is reprehensible!"

Andrina drew in her breath sharply.

"I hate you!" she declared, without considering her words.

The Duke looked over her shoulder.

"As I see your ardent admirer approaching, I suggest you straighten your wreath and that we will, with something approaching dignity, go into the Ball-Room."

Andrina's hands, which were trembling, went to her head. Then with what she hoped was a dignified grace she moved towards the open window.

She was well aware that the Duke was frowning and he was still angry with her, but she was at the same time grateful that he was preventing her from having to speak to Lord Crowhurst again.

There was no doubt, she told herself later that night, that the Duke and Lord Crowhurst between them had spoilt the Ball for her.

She had managed to dance, to smile, and to make herself pleasant to a countless number of people.

She had accepted the Prince Regent's congratulations on her appearance, conveyed to her in the flirtatious but charming manner that was all his own, and yet she had only felt miserable.

The gaiety and sparkle had gone out of the evening.

It was some consolation, when the last guest had departed long after dawn had broken, to hear both Cheryl and Sharon exclaiming that it was the most wonderful, perfect party there had ever been!

"I always dreamt of a Ball like that," Sharon said, "but I never thought I would go to one, and if you had told me even a month ago that it would be given for us I would have known I was dreaming!"

"We were very proud of you all, were we not, Tancred?" Lady Evelyn asked.

"Of course," he replied. "I was effusively congratulated on having been so clever or so lucky as to find such attractive and well-behaved Wards!"

Although her sisters were delighted with the compliment, Andrina knew that the Duke was being sarcastic deliberately.

"You must go to bed at once, girls," Lady Evelyn said. "I cannot have you looking pale tomorrow night, and we have a Reception to attend in the afternoon."

"How exciting!" Sharon exclaimed.

Cheryl curtseyed to Lady Evelyn, then to the Duke, and turned towards the stairs. Andrina followed to slip her arm through her younger sister's and asked softly:

"You have been happy, dearest?"

"It has been a wonderful evening!" Cheryl replied.

"I saw you dancing with the Marquis. You liked dancing with him?"

"He was very kind."

There was something in Cheryl's tone that told Andrina she did not wish to discuss it further, and, having taken her to her bedroom, where there was a sleepy maid waiting to help her undress, Andrina went to find Sharon.

Her youngest sister was waltzing dreamily round and round her bed-room.

"Oh, Andrina," she said, "could anybody have had a more perfect, more marvellous, more glorious evening?"

"Did you dance with the Duke?" Andrina asked.

Sharon stopped waltzing and walked towards the dressing-table.

"Of course, I did as you told me."

"What did you talk to him about?"

Sharon did not answer and after a moment Andrina said:

"You know what I want, Sharon. He is a difficult man, but if anyone could charm him into a good mood, if anyone could make him into an acceptable husband, it is you!"

Sharon was still silent, then after a moment she said:

"Do you suppose that being a Duchess would really make one happy?"

"But of course it would," Andrina said quickly. "You would have everything—this wonderful house, all the jewels we saw tonight, and the Duke has many other possessions we have not yet seen: his house in the country about which Papa used to talk, a Hunting Lodge in Leicester, and a house at Newmarket where he stays for the races."

Andrina paused and after a moment continued:

"I have never seen Cheryl so gay as she seemed tonight with the Marquis, and if you were both Duchesses, think what an achievement that would be!"

"The Duke was not a particularly amusing partner," Sharon said after a moment.

"You have to charm and fascinate him, Sharon. After all, if he had been easy he would have been married before now. Think of all the women who must have wanted to be the Duchess of Broxbourne! But I am quite certain that none of them was as beautiful as you!"

Sharon gave a little yawn.

"I am tired, Andrina."

"Of course you are," Andrina replied, "and it is selfish of me to want to talk. Go to sleep. There are lots of exciting things to do tomorrow. But, Sharon, just remember one thing: we have very little time."

When she was in her own room and the maid had taken away her Ball-gown, dressed only in her thin night-gown Andrina walked to the window.

She pulled aside the curtains.

The pale morning sun was already climbing up the sky, shining on the roofs, and glittering on the window-panes of the houses that she could just see beyond the drive.

"So little time," she whispered, and yet somehow she had to marry Cheryl to the Marquis and Sharon to the Duke.

She could not help feeling that the latter might prove an impossible task, and yet, she told herself, she was determined—completely and utterly determined—that she would do her best for her sisters.

That was why she had come to London. That was why she had sacrificed her pride to plead and beg the Duke to make them his protégées.

Then she remembered the contempt and anger in his voice tonight.

How could he have said such things to her?

'He despises me,' she thought, 'and he has told me often enough that I am brainless, idiotic, and in his eyes unprincipled.'

She felt a surge of anger once again that he could accuse her of such things, and yet she had to admit that when she had come from the garden he had some excuse for his comments.

It had been crazy of her to let the Earl take her into the arbour. She ought to have refused to leave the Ball-Room with him in the first place and should have allowed Cheryl, as she had supposed the unknown girl to be, to look after herself.

"I suppose I am very . . . foolish," Andrina admitted humbly.

Then as she put her head down on the pillow she thought she would not have to endure the Duke with his suspicions and his innuendos for long.

The moment Cheryl and Sharon were safely married she would be free of him.

Yet she wished that before that time came she could prove him wrong, confound him in some way so that he would be sorry not only for the things he had said to her but also for his behaviour when they had first met.

"How can I make him respect me?" she asked herself, and found that there was no answer to that question.

*   *   *

The following day it was late before anyone was aroused from sleep, and actually it was Andrina who came downstairs first to find the Hall filled with flowers of every description.

There were bouquets, baskets, bowls, and sprays addressed in almost equal numbers to Cheryl and Sharon, and, to her surprise, some for herself.

There were two magnificent bouquets from the gentlemen who had sat at either side of her at dinner, two from gentlemen she could not remember, and one huge basket of white orchids, of which she knew the donor before she opened the note.

The Earl's writing was like himself, Andrina thought, dark, uneven, and somehow slightly sinister.

"To Andrina who has captured both my heart and mind."

She tore up the card and threw it in the waste-paper basket.

'I cannot think why the one man in London I really dislike should be the one who pursues me,' Andrina thought.

"You have certainly all been a sensation as far as floral tributes are concerned," Lady Evelyn said when she appeared just before luncheon, "but flowers die. What you girls need is something lasting."

"What is that?" Cheryl asked.

"An engagement-ring!" Lady Evelyn replied. "Preferably of diamonds!"

"Oh, an engagement-ring," Cheryl said, and there was something in the way she spoke which made Andrina look at her sharply.

Could the Marquis have said anything last night? she wondered.

She did not wish to press her younger sister, but she felt excitedly that Cheryl was undoubtedly thinking of marriage, and it was obvious that the only man she could have in mind was the Marquis.

Sharon collected the cards from her flowers immediately after luncheon and put them away in a little satin reticule she carried on her arm.

"Are you not going to tell us the names of your admirers?" Lady Evelyn enquired.

"I am too tired to worry about them now," Sharon said in a voice which did not sound as if she was at all tired, "but later this afternoon I shall have to write and thank them."

"I think we can forget about 'thank you' letters for today," Lady Evelyn said. "I thought we might go driving."

"That would be lovely!" Andrina said. "But first I had better take the jewellery we borrowed last night back to Mr. Robson."

She put the stars that Sharon had worn in her hair and the necklace which had encircled Cheryl's white neck back in their boxes and went along the corridor to Mr. Robson's office.

"Thank you very much, Miss Andrina," he said, taking the jewellery from her. "It is very kind of you to be so prompt in returning them. I do not mind telling you it worries me when such things are not safely in my keeping. The Duke trusts me, and if anything was lost I should have no-one to blame but myself."

"That is a horrible feeling, as we all know," Andrina smiled.

"May I tell you how beautiful you looked last night, Miss Andrina?" Mr. Robson asked. "I thought, as I watched you dancing, you had been quite right in thinking you needed no jewels. They would only have been dimmed by the excitement in your eyes!"

Because he was an elderly man Andrina did not feel it was impertinent of him to speak in such a manner.

"Thank you very much," she said. "I thought no-one would be looking at me when my sisters were in the Ball-Room. At the same time, everyone was very kind."

'With the exception of the Duke!' she added to herself.

He had not only failed to pay her a compliment, he had actually abused her and once again aroused her anger.

She talked to Mr. Robson for a little while about the other guests, and he told her how much he admired Lady Cowper and how everyone in her employment worshipped her.

Then Andrina had returned to the Salon to find Lady Evelyn alone.

"Have Cheryl and Sharon gone to get ready to go driving?" Andrina asked.

"They have already gone," Lady Evelyn said.

"Gone?" Andrina questioned.

"The Marquis of Glen called for Cheryl. Apparently they had arranged that he should do so last evening," Lady Evelyn explained.

"You let her go alone?" Andrina enquired.

"My dear, he was driving a *vis-à-vis*, which, as you well know, only provides for two occupants. I could hardly sit on the driver's lap, nor could you expect Cheryl to sit on mine!"

Lady Evelyn laughed as she went on:

"Stop looking like a worried hen who has lost her chicks, Andrina! Cheryl and Sharon are perfectly all right and it is entirely *convenable*, I assure you, for girls to go driving in the afternoon, providing they keep to the popular parts of Hyde Park."

"And with whom has Sharon gone?" Andrina asked.

She knew even as she asked the question what the answer would be.

"Who else but the handsome Count Ivan?" Lady Evelyn replied. "I saw last night that he was very enamoured, and I must say he is one of the most attractive men I have ever met."

"He is not at all suitable for Sharon," Andrina said sharply, "and I hope, Ma'am, you will not encourage this association. I thought she danced with him far too frequently at the Ball."

Lady Evelyn said nothing and after a moment Andrina went on:

"You yourself told me that he was looking for a rich heiress. I think he should be warned, before things go too far, that Sharon is absolutely penniless."

There was a smile on Lady Evelyn's lips as she said:

"You sound exactly like my mother. That is the way she talked when I was a girl, and yet I married my husband and we were very happy!"

She saw Andrina's expression and said:

"He became an Ambassador and made a great success of his career. When I first met him he was no-one of any importance, with little influence and nothing to recommend him even in the Diplomatic Service except that he had an aptitude for languages."

"I want Sharon to make a good marriage," Andrina said. "I am quite sure, Ma'am, that Count Ivan Birkendorff is not the type of husband we would want for her."

"I am sure you know best, Andrina," Lady Evelyn answered, "but do not forget that the last word rests with the Duke."

"Why is that?" Andrina enquired. "I am looking after my sisters."

"On the contrary," Lady Evelyn replied, "we have proclaimed to the world that you are the Duke's Wards. Therefore, if any young man wishes to lay his hand and his heart at your feet, he has first, as you are all under twenty-one, to ask your Guardian's permission."

"I should have thought that was unnecessary," Andrina said quickly.

Lady Evelyn shook her head.

"Most young men would be extremely nervous of doing the wrong thing, especially in the eyes of someone like the Duke of Broxbourne. His Grace, as we both know, can be very autocratic when it suits him, and I have a feeling that any suitor of whom he does not approve will be very quickly shown the outside of the front door."

"Do you think I should speak to the Duke about this?" Andrina asked reluctantly.

"I think you will find that he is your strongest defence," Lady Evelyn replied. "At the same time, he will undoubtedly have his own ideas on the subject."

"We can be quite sure of that!" Andrina said bitterly, remembering the way the Duke had spoken to her last night.

"I still think you must have cast a spell on him," Lady Evelyn said. "After all these years during which no Ball has been given in this house and Tancred has only entertained his own particular friends."

She laughed and went on:

"When I think how he has lived up to his reputation of being difficult and inhospitable, I can hardly believe this is really happening!"

"It was a lovely Ball," Andrina said without much enthusiasm in her voice.

"I saw you dancing with the Earl of Crowhurst," Lady Evelyn said. "Now, if you can bring him up to scratch, that would be a great achievement!"

"No!" Andrina said vehemently. "No! I assure you,

Ma'am, that he is not really interested in me, nor I in him!"

She walked from the Salon as she spoke and did not realise that Lady Evelyn gave a knowing little laugh as the door shut firmly behind her.

CHAPTER FIVE

Andrina returned to the house with Lady Evelyn after attending a Reception which secretly she had found rather dull.

It had been full of Her Ladyship's friends and, although they had been kind and flatteringly inquisitive, Andrina was well aware that what they really wanted was to gossip about the Duke.

It had obviously caused a sensation that after all these years he had suddenly entertained on such a lavish scale, and she sensed that the *Beau Monde* were already speculating as to which of his attractive Wards he would marry.

She wondered if in fact Sharon had done as she had advised her and gone out of her way to be charming and fascinating to him.

"Of course," Andrina told herself with a sigh, "Sharon is very young."

At the same time, it was impossible to think of the Duke being married to Cheryl.

As she returned to Broxbourne House in the Duke's comfortable London carriage with Lady Evelyn chattering beside her, Andrina was wondering whether she would find on arrival that Cheryl had received a proposal of marriage from the Marquis.

He had certainly singled her out, both at the Ball last night and by taking her driving alone in the Park. But when she remembered that Sharon had also gone driving with the Count, it overshadowed her pleasure about Cheryl.

"You are very silent, Andrina," Lady Evelyn said when she had asked a question and received no answer.

"I am sorry, Ma'am, if I appear rude," Andrina answered. "I was thinking of Cheryl and Sharon and wondering if they will have returned."

"I am sure they will have done so," Lady Evelyn said, "and you will doubtless find them both having tea in the Salon."

Unfortunately this hope did not materialise.

There was no-one in the Salon when Andrina arrived at Broxbourne House and she learnt to her consternation that neither Cheryl nor Sharon had returned from their drive.

"How could they be so long?" she asked.

"Time does not exist when one is young," Lady Evelyn said blithely and went upstairs to change.

Andrina was just about to follow her when the Butler said:

"His Grace is in the Library, Miss, and wished to see you when you returned."

Andrina felt her heart give a frightened throb.

Was the Duke still angry with her, as he had been last night?

She had a sudden terror that perhaps he was so incensed that he was unwilling to continue entertaining them, and intended to send them away.

Then she thought that she was alarming herself unnecessarily.

He had been angry, it was true, but it was not Cheryl's or Sharon's fault and she had the feeling that, difficult though he was, he would be just. Yet, she asked herself, what grounds had she for thinking that?

She knew nothing about him, nothing at all except that he was overpowering, autocratic, and at times infuriating.

'Where he is concerned, I always seem to do the wrong thing, she thought.

Then her pride made her add:

'Why should it trouble me? Once Cheryl and Sharon are married, I will never see him again.'

However, feeling that it would be unwise to keep the Duke waiting, she took off her bonnet and the light silk pelise she had worn over a pretty muslin gown and gave them to the Butler.

Then holding her head high she walked along the corridor to the Library.

A footman opened the door for her and she went in to find the Duke at his desk.

He half rose as she entered, then seated himself again and indicated with his hand a chair on the other side of the desk.

Andrina looked at him and thought he was looking more cynical than usual, and she saw too that he still looked angry and there was a frown between his eyes.

She felt her spirits sink; then once again she told herself defiantly that she would not be overpowered by him.

Because she was nervous she spoke quickly as she said:

"I think before I hear what you wish to say to me, Your Grace, I should thank you in all sincerity for your great kindness in giving the Ball last night."

She paused. The Duke made no reply and Andrina went on:

"Everyone today has been saying it was the best party they ever attended and that Broxbourne House never looked more magnificent!"

Still the Duke did not speak, and after a moment, because his silence was so nerve-racking, Andrina said in a low voice:

"Why did Your Grace . . . want to see . . . me?"

"I wished to congratulate you, Andrina. You have been more astute than I expected or gave you credit for."

"About what?" Andrina asked.

"As if you did not know!" he replied scornfully. "Let me make it easier by telling you that your 'ardent admirer' called to see you after you had left the house."

"I have no idea what you are talking about," Andrina answered, but the colour rose in her cheeks.

"As I have already said, I must congratulate you," the Duke went on. "From a wordly point of view it is a brilliant match, and it will put you in a position where you can look after your sisters, as you have not been able to do in the past."

Andrina's eyes were on the Duke's face. Then she said, hardly above a whisper:

"What . . . are you . . . trying to . . . tell me?"

"I am informing you," the Duke said, "that the Earl of Crowhurst has asked for your hand in marriage, and as your Guardian I have naturally given him my consent!"

For a moment Andrina felt as if her heart had stopped beating and she was paralysed.

Then without thinking what she was doing she rose to her feet and walked across the room to the window to stand staring out at the garden bathed in sunshine.

"You have achieved what you set out to do," the Duke's voice said behind her. "Crowhurst is a matrimonial catch, as my cousin Evelyn will be able to assure you in more detail than I can."

Andrina did not move.

She was remembering how last night when the Earl had touched her she had felt disgusted and revolted to the point where she longed to scream.

She recalled how she had fought herself free of him, and how frightened she had been that his superior strength would hold her captive despite all her efforts to escape.

When she went to bed she had scrubbed violently with soap and water the places on her shoulder and on her neck where he had kissed her. Even then, lying in the darkness she could feel the hot insistence of his mouth.

She had told the Duke that she hated him, but it was

a very different hatred from that which she felt for
Lord Crowhurst.

The Duke angered her and she fought him mentally.
But what she felt for Lord Crowhurst was entirely
physical, the shrinking of her whole body when he
came near her, as if from something evil and unclean.

"I am waiting, Andrina," the Duke said.

Andrina turned from the window.

"Please," she said in a voice that he could hardly
hear. "I . . . cannot . . . marry him!"

There was a moment's silence. Then the Duke said:

"Am I hearing you a-right, Andrina? Are you telling
me you do not wish to marry His Lordship?"

"I . . . cannot do . . . so," she answered, and still her
voice seemed strangled in her throat.

The Duke rose to walk to the mantelpiece and stood
with his back to it.

"As your Guardian," he said, "I must point out the
advantages this marriage would bring you."

Andrina would have turned back to the garden
again, but he said sharply:

"You will listen to me, Andrina! Come and sit
down!"

Slowly and reluctantly she obeyed him, crossing the
floor to seat herself on a chair at the side of the hearth.

She thought as she did so that to sit beside the Duke
when he was standing made him seem even larger and
more overpowering.

Because she knew she must obey him she clasped
her hands together in her lap and waited.

"The Earl is not only a very rich man," the Duke
began after a moment, "but he is also accepted in the
most exclusive circles. He is well-known in the field of
sport and he has one of the best racing-stables in England."

He paused before he went on:

"He has also—which from a woman's point of view,
it appears, is important—fallen in love with you; in
fact he was quite lyrical about your attractions."

There was a sarcastic note in the Duke's voice which made Andrina wince.

It was quite obvious, she thought, that he did not share the Earl's sentiments.

"You came to London to find a husband."

Andrina made a little gesture of protest, but he continued before she could speak:

"Oh, I know the pretext was that you were concerned only with your two sisters. But you must have realised there were men who would be interested in you as well. And so, Andrina, you have managed to pick the ripest peach from the very top of the tree!"

Again there was a note in the Duke's voice which made her feel as if he flicked her with a whip.

Then clasping her hands so tightly that her fingers were white she said:

"It is no . . . use. I understand all the . . . advantages. I know how much I could . . . help Cheryl and Sharon, but I cannot marry him . . . I cannot!"

Her voice broke on a little sob.

There was silence until the Duke asked in a different voice:

"Will you give me a reason?"

"I do not . . . love . . . him!"

He could hardly hear the words, and yet they were spoken.

"Love?" the Duke ejaculated, and his voice seemed to echo round the Library. "Love, Andrina? This is the first time you have ever mentioned that illusory emotion. I thought it was position you wanted, a title and a coronet to wear on your pretty head! Those things seldom go hand in hand with love!"

'He is right,' Andrina thought.

She had been so intent on seeking what she thought was best for Cheryl and Sharon that she had forgotten that marriage was not only the house one lived in, the name one took, or the Social position one achieved; it also meant living with a man.

But how, without love, could one tolerate the closeness and intimacy of it?

There was a silence for some moments before the Duke said:

"I am waiting, Andrina, for you to explain this sudden change in your aspirations. Can it be that you yourself have fallen in love?"

"No . . . no . . . of course not!" Andrina answered quickly. "It is just . . . that I know I could never . . . marry the Earl, not if he was the . . . last man alive!"

She spoke passionately and the Duke with his eyes on her face said quietly:

"Love sometimes comes after marriage. You have not known him long."

"He is horrible!" Andrina cried. "There is something about him which . . . frightens me. I could not . . . let him . . . touch me again."

"He touched you?"

The Duke's question was sharp.

"He kissed my . . . shoulder and my . . . neck," Andrina murmured. "I thought I would be . . . unable to . . . escape from . . . him."

The Duke could hear the terror in her voice. Then he said drily:

"You were exceedingly successful in extricating yourself from the same position where I was concerned!"

"That was . . . different."

"Why?"

She could not answer him, for she did not know herself why she had not been frightened when he had kissed her.

She had been shocked, surprised, angry at his audacity; but she had not been frightened as she had been by the Earl, nor had she felt revolted and disgusted by the touch of his lips.

In fact, she could remember that strange sensation, unlike anything she had ever known before, which had certainly not been disgust but something very different.

With an effort Andrina rose to her feet.

"Will Your Grace thank the Earl of Crowhurst for

his offer," she said, "and inform him that I cannot . . . accept it?"

"You are sure of what you are saying?" the Duke remarked. "You do not think, Andrina, that you would be wise to accept the Earl, knowing you are unlikely to get a better offer?"

"I am quite certain! I would rather remain unmarried for the rest of my life!" Andrina said violently.

"Very well," the Duke said. "I will send a groom with a note to His Lordship, and I will try to ensure that he does not trouble you in the future."

"Please do . . . that," Andrina pleaded. "I could not . . . bear to meet him . . . again."

"I cannot promise that that will not happen," the Duke answered, "but at least he shall not trouble you in this house. If you meet in anyone else's, do not go into the garden with him!"

Andrina blushed.

"It was unnecessary for you to add . . . that, Your Grace."

"You have a habit of being forgetful in such matters," the Duke replied.

She would have left him, then she remembered that she had in fact wished to see him about Sharon.

"I think, Your Grace," she said, "I should inform you that I am not pleased at the manner in which Count Ivan Birkendorff is pursuing Sharon. I do not consider him to be suitable as a husband, and I should be grateful if you would persuade him to interest himself elsewhere."

"Has Sharon asked you to speak to me about this?" the Duke enquired.

"No, of course not," Andrina replied. "Sharon is young and impetuous, and of course the Count is very handsome, but there is no point in her wasting time with him."

"Of course not, if he is not to be allowed to offer her anything but a transitory amusement," the Duke agreed solemnly.

"There is certainly no time for that," Andrina said.

"Your Grace is aware that when we have spent our money we shall have to return to the country. Before that happens, both Cheryl and Sharon must be married!"

"I quite see you must concentrate on the serious business of finding husbands."

Andrina knew that the Duke was laughing at her and she answered crossly:

"It may be a joke to Your Grace, but for Cheryl and Sharon their happiness depends entirely on what happens in these next few weeks. They are care-free and impulsive. I have to think for them."

"And yet you are not prepared to sacrifice yourself on their behalf?"

Andrina raised her eyes to his and he saw how worried they were.

"That is what I know I ... ought to ... do, but ... it is ... impossible for me."

"I beg your pardon, Andrina," the Duke said unexpectedly. "You have made your decision and I should not have mentioned it again. Forget it, and stop fussing unnecessarily over your sisters. All three of you are young and very beautiful. Make the most of your success while you can. Tomorrow will take care of itself."

"That is a gambler's outlook, Your Grace," Andrina flashed.

"Then have a gambler's faith that you will turn up the right card," the Duke replied.

He smiled, and she thought that he looked kinder and more sympathetic than he had ever done before as he said:

"Leave everything to me, you foolish child! If you trust me, I will find solutions to your problems."

"I do trust you," Andrina said instinctively, and was surprised at herself for saying so. Then she added:

"I am sorry ... Your Grace, if I was ... rude last night. You have been so kind, more kind than I could ever have expected or hoped. I am ... ashamed that I have not behaved as you would have wished me to do."

The Duke smiled again.

"You behave somewhat unpredictably, Andrina! But what woman ever does anything else?"

Andrina did not quite know what to make of this remark, but she thought about it long after she had left him.

She found that Cheryl had now returned and was upstairs, taking off her bonnet.

"You are very late, Cheryl!" Andrina said.

"It was so nice in the Park," Cheryl answered in a dreamy voice. "And we watched the ducks swimming on the Serpentine."

"What did you talk about?" Andrina asked tentatively.

"Oh, lots of things."

Andrina was longing to question her further; but it appeared that Cheryl had rung the bell, for her maid came into the room and there was no chance to say anything intimate.

Instead Andrina went in search of Sharon, only to find that she was with Lady Evelyn, and for the rest of the evening she seemed, Andrina thought, to deliberately avoid the chance of a private chat.

She could only hope that the Duke would do as she had asked and prevent the Count from wasting any more of Sharon's time.

He was so good-looking and from all reports quite clever; so it was natural that Sharon would be dazzled not only by his handsome countenance but also by his typically Russian aura of glamour, which one did not find in English gentlemen.

"She will soon forget him." Andrina told herself. "Tomorrow I will talk to her again about making herself pleasant to the Duke."

And if it was not the Duke, she went on in her mind, there were obviously a number of gentlemen who had sent flowers and who made their way quickly to Sharon's side the moment she appeared at any party.

Now that she was free of Lord Crowhurst, Andrina felt as if a cloud that had been overshadowing her ever since last night had been lifted and she was in the sunshine again.

They went out to dinner and danced afterwards, but the Duke did not accompany them. As it was a party given for some very young people, Andrina felt almost as if she were one of the Dowagers.

Watching the young men dancing with Cheryl and Sharon, she thought they all looked very immature and told herself it was because, even though he infuriated her and they seemed to fight whenever they met, there was something stimulating in fencing with a man as sophisticated and intelligent as the Duke.

She wondered what had made him so cynical and thought perhaps Lady Evelyn would know the answer to that question.

Sometime in his life he must have been young and ardent and full of laughter.

Why had he changed and why, when he was so richly endowed with a great position and magnificent possessions, did he go out of his way to be ironic and sarcastic?

It was a problem she could not solve, but she went to bed thinking of the Duke and when she awoke in the morning she had an uneasy feeling that she had dreamt of him.

*   *   *

The ladies of Broxbourne House breakfasted in an attractive Boudoir which was situated between their bed-rooms.

It was fragrant with the scent of flowers from the bouquets and baskets-full they had been given, and Andrina entered to find Cheryl looking exquisitely lovely in a white muslin negligé, her fair hair falling over her shoulders.

"I slept so late," she said with a smile, "I thought you would not mind if I had breakfast before I dressed."

"Of course not, dearest," Andrina answered. "There is no hurry in the mornings, thank goodness. We seem to be on the run all day."

"Tonight there is a dance at the Russian Embassy," Sharon said with a sudden lilt in her voice that Andrina did not miss.

"I had not forgotten," Lady Evelyn exclaimed as she entered the room. "The Princess de Lieven has asked us all to dine, which I can tell you is a very great honour. Her Highness normally has no use for young girls."

"I wonder who could have persuaded her to make an exception where we are concerned?" Sharon said with a hint of mischief in her eyes.

As Andrina knew the answer to that, she said quickly:

"I see you both have quite a number of letters. Is not that exciting? At home if we received a letter once a month it was an event!"

Cheryl was opening one of her letters and Andrina had seen the crest on the back of the envelope and knew who had sent it.

Then suddenly Cheryl gave a little cry.

"Oh, no!" she cried.

"What is it?" Andrina enquired.

Without replying, Cheryl rose and, throwing the letter down onto the table, ran from the room.

Andrina picked it up and read:

I have been told not to see you again by 'He who must be Obeyed' where you are concerned. But this is just to tell you, my darling, that I love you with all my heart and I shall never love anyone else.

There has never been anyone so beautiful as you, and although I may not see you, your face will always be before my eyes.

Andrina read it incredulously not once but twice, and there was no need to read the address on the top of the writing-paper to know who had sent it.

"What is it? What has happened?" Lady Evelyn asked.

Without replying, Andrina, holding the letter in her hand, opened the Boudoir door and ran downstairs.

She knew that the Duke breakfasted in the Morning-Room, but when she approached it she saw that the door was open and knew he would have finished and gone into the Library.

He was there standing on the hearth-rug, with *The Times* newspaper open in his hands.

He looked up as she appeared, then shut the newspaper and laid it down on an adjacent table.

Andrina walked across the room towards him and held out the letter which Cheryl had received.

"Will you explain this?" she asked.

The Duke took it from her without haste, read it, and handed it back.

"As you must have guessed," he said, "I have told the noble Marquis to leave Cheryl alone."

"Why? Why?" Andrina asked.

"For reasons I do not think it fair to tell you," the Duke answered. "You must accept my judgment in the matter."

"I have no intention of doing anything of the sort!" Andrina answered angrily. "Cheryl very much likes the Marquis. It is obvious that he loves her. Why should they not get married? Why should you interfere?"

There was silence. Then the Duke said:

"You are making this rather difficult for me, Andrina, and I should have prevented Glen from sending that over-dramatic letter to Cheryl. It will of course upset her quite unnecessarily, but frankly, although I think she was flattered by his attentions, I do not believe her heart is really involved."

"Cheryl likes the Marquis," Andrina replied, "and if he wishes to marry her I have every intention of allowing them to do so."

"You need my permission."

"That is nonsense, as you well know!" Andrina

snapped. "I forced you against your better judgment into constituting yourself our Guardian. You said it was a crazy scheme, and you wished to have little part in it. Now you are interfering, giving orders, preventing us from doing what we wish to do. Cheryl will marry the Marquis!"

"I think you will find that the Marquis will not ask her," the Duke said firmly.

Andrina stamped her foot.

"He loves her! He says so in this letter! But it is obvious that you have put some pressure on him and he is afraid of you."

The Duke did not answer and Andrina said:

"Very well, I am going to find the Marquis now at this moment. I am going to tell him you have no jurisdiction over us, whatsoever, and if he wishes to marry Cheryl he may do so!"

She turned to leave the room but the Duke put out his hand and caught her wrist.

"Listen to me. I have a reason, a very good reason why Cheryl cannot marry the Marquis."

"I do not believe you," Andrina said angrily.

"Please trust me, Andrina."

The Duke was pleading with her, but she was too angry to listen.

"You are just being tyrannical and autocratic, as you have been before," she stormed. "You do not want to do what is best for Cheryl and you do not want her to be a Duchess! You are being deliberately obstinate for no reason, except in order to show your power. I am going to see the Marquis, and nothing you can do or say will stop me!"

She twisted her arm but the Duke still kept his hand firmly on her wrist. Then he said quietly:

"If you persist in making a fool of yourself, I suppose I shall have to tell you the reason why I have told the Marquis he cannot marry Cheryl."

"What is it? . . . if you have any reason!" Andrina demanded.

"He is already married!"

Andrina was still, the anger fading from her eyes.

"How can that be true? And if it is, why does no-one know about it?"

"Sit down, Andrina," the Duke said. "I did not wish to tell you this because it concerns only the Marquis, and he is in fact more sinned against than sinning. But I have to make you understand."

He released her wrist and because she suddenly felt weak Andrina sat down on a chair.

"Is that really the truth?" she asked.

"Nine years ago, when he first went up to Oxford," the Duke said, "the Marquis got in with a riotous and fast set. They used to come up to London regularly during the term and enjoy themselves in Nightclubs of doubtful repute."

He paused to go on slowly;

"After one very drunken evening Glen found he had married a woman with whom he had been enjoying himself, although he had little memory of it."

"They were . . . really married?" Andrina asked in a low voice.

"She stage-managed the whole thing, knowing who the Marquis was. The Parson, although he was a reprobate, was nevertheless in Holy Orders, and the Marriage-Certificate was genuine."

The Duke sighed before he continued:

"The Arkraes were naturally appalled when they heard what had occurred, but a divorce would have caused a great scandal. As you know, it requires an Act of Parliament."

"What did they do?" Andrina asked.

"They paid the woman a large sum of money to go abroad and not return to this country. Two years later they announced to their family and their immediate friends that she had died."

Andrina's eyes lit up.

"Then if she is dead," she said, "the Marquis is free."

"That is what he himself believed," the Duke re-

plied, "but unfortunately I met his wife when I was in
Brussels after the Battle of Waterloo."

"How could you have met her?" Andrina asked in a
hostile voice, as if she did not believe him.

"I was celebrating our victory with several of my
brother-officers," the Duke replied, "and when I saw
the proprietress of the *Maison de Plaisir* in which we
were amusing ourselves, I felt sure that I had seen her
before."

"Where had you done that?" Andrina asked.

"I was one of the party of undergraduates who came
to London from Oxford the night that Glen was married!"

"You were there?"

The Duke nodded.

"I was there!"

"Then why did you not prevent it?"

"There were at least a dozen of us present," the
Duke replied. "but I was older than Glen, and not a
particular friend of his. Frankly, no-one had any idea
that this woman, who was in those days most attractive, had anything like marriage in mind."

He smiled a little cynically before he added:

"We were all considerably 'foxed' by the end of the
evening!"

"Are you sure it was the same woman you saw in
Brussels?" Andrina asked. "What was she doing in a
House of . . . Pleasure?"

The Duke paused for a moment, then he said:

"She owned it!"

"What happened there?" Andrina asked. "Was it a
place where you could gamble?"

Again the Duke paused before he replied:

"That—sort of thing!"

"And you are quite certain it was the same person?"

"As a matter of fact she remembered me, or I would
not have been able to place her," the Duke answered.
"She had altered considerably, and it was not for the
better! In fact I doubt very much if she will live long;

she was coughing blood and, although I am not a Doctor, I am sure she has a wasting disease!"

"But the Marquis is still married?"

"He is still married," the Duke affirmed, "although he does not wish to think so."

"It is too cruel . . . too unfair!" Andrina exclaimed.

"I agree with you," the Duke said quietly. "At the same time, there is nothing you can do about it."

"No, I realise that," Andrina said, "and I had been so certain that Cheryl would be happy with him. She does not like many men. She is frightened of them, but she got on well with the Marquis."

"He would certainly frighten no-one!" the Duke said with a touch of sarcasm in his voice. "At the same time, I am not certain that if two such ineffectual people married they would deal well together. I cannot imagine Cheryl running a big Castle in Scotland or taking over from the Duchess, who has a very distinct and domineering personality."

"You do not have to be domineering to be a Duchess," Andrina replied.

"There are certain duties which are expected from a Ducal family," the Duke replied, "especially in Scotland, where the Chief of the Clan reigns almost as a King."

Andrina had to admit to herself that Cheryl would find this difficult, but she did not wish to give the Duke the satisfaction of hearing her admit he was right.

"So there is nothing we can do, Your Grace?" she said. "I suppose now I shall have to try to find someone else for Cheryl. It is most unfortunate: she has wasted so much time already with the Marquis."

"That is undoubtedly a catastrophe," the Duke remarked.

There was a twinkle in his eye and Andrina knew he was laughing at her.

"It is all very well for you to talk like that," she said hotly, "but money does not last forever."

She thought he would say something scathing in reply and so before he could answer her she turned and went from the room, shutting the door noisily behind her.

She went upstairs to Cheryl's bed-room to find her sister sitting moodily in a chair.

"Are you very upset, darling?" she asked.

"I liked him," Cheryl said, "and he loves me, he told me so! Why has the Duke sent him away?"

"I think he thought that you would find it difficult to be the Duchess of Arkrae," Andrina replied quickly. "They have an enormous Castle and vast estates in Scotland, and the Duke and Duchess are treated almost like Royalty. I would like to think of you reigning there, Cheryl, but would it have made you happy?"

Cheryl shook her head.

"I did not think of it like that," she said. "The Marquis is quiet and gentle, but I would be frightened of meeting crowds of people. You know I do not like that sort of thing."

"Yes, I know, dearest," Andrina said, "and therefore perhaps it is for the best that he should go away now, rather than if you had fallen in love with him."

"He was very nice," Cheryl said wistfully, "but he did not say very much."

"Try to forget him," Andrina begged. "The Duke is wise in such matters and he was sure you would not be happy."

"That was kind of him," Cheryl said. "I had forgotten that the Marquis will eventually become a Duke. If I had to run a house as big as this, I could never manage, I know I could not!"

"But you would have lots of servants to do it for you," Andrina said reassuringly.

"It is too big!" Cheryl said positively.

Andrina was relieved that her heart seemed not too involved. At the same time, she could not help thinking that it was a tragedy that Cheryl could not marry the Marquis and, whatever the Duke might say, she was sure they would have been content together.

Now she had to start all over again finding a hus-

band for Cheryl and she knew it would not be an easy
task, despite her sister's acknowledged beauty.

Sharon and Lady Evelyn were naturally extremely
curious as to why the Duke had sent the Marquis
away.

"I am not allowed to tell you the reason," Andrina
said loftily. "You will have to ask the Duke yourselves."

She was quite certain that neither of them would
presume to do so, and while they tried to persuade her
to tell them secretly, she would not be drawn, feeling it
was not fair to the Marquis, for whom she had the
deepest sympathy.

She could not help wondering, however, if the Duke
had enjoyed himself in the House of Pleasure in Brussels.

Perhaps when he was with the type of woman he
would meet there he was more relaxed, less aloof, and
probably less cynical; but that was something she
would never know for certain, she told herself.

Lady Evelyn had some shopping to do and asked
Andrina to accompany her.

Sharon said she had some letters to write and Cheryl
said she was too tired.

They therefore had a very early luncheon, before
Andrina and Lady Evelyn set off for the shops.

Andrina had made up her mind that they must
spend no more money on clothes unless it was absolutely necessary.

She was quite certain that already they must have
spent a great deal of their five hundred pounds, and
she thought that once again she must ask the Duke to
render her an account so that she would know exactly
what they had left.

Nevertheless, there was a gown in Madame Bertin's
that was irresistible. In white gossamer net, it was exactly the sort of dress in which Cheryl would look angelic, and Andrina thought perhaps it would cheer her
up if she took it home with her as a present.

Madame Bertin was only too willing to oblige, and it

did not take long to have it packed and placed in the carriage.

They set off driving back through the crowded streets which never ceased to amuse and interest Andrina almost as if they were a theatrical performance, staged especially for her benefit.

"I cannot believe that anywhere else in the world one can see such smart people or such magnificent horses," she said to Lady Evelyn.

"You are right there," Lady Evelyn replied. "I have, as you know, travelled a great deal, and my husband and I always said that for real elegance there was nowhere like London, especially in the Season."

"Of course, we are only looking at the best parts of it," Andrina said. I have heard terrible stories of the slums and of what goes on in St. Giles and other places like it."

"My dear, it is no use troubling yourself with such matters," Lady Evelyn said. "I can promise you that in that respect London is not half as bad as Rome, or even Paris!"

'It is bad enough,' Andrina told herself.

She had heard stories of the Flash Houses where thieves and child pick-pockets herded together in places so rough that no respectable person would dare to go near them.

She had read reports in newspapers of the cruelty with which some apprentices were treated, and she longed to support those who were fighting for the abolition of the young chimney-sweeps—"The Climbing Boys" as they were called.

She wondered if the Duke ever concerned himself with such matters, then told herself that Lady Evelyn was assuredly right and he was too selfish and egotistical ever to be concerned with anyone or anything except himself.

They arrived home and as she walked into the Hall Andrina said to the Butler:

"Is Miss Cheryl downstairs?"

"No, Miss. Miss Cheryl has gone driving."

"I thought she was going to rest!" Andrina exclaimed. "With whom did she go?"

"With the Marquis of Glen, Miss. He called soon after you had left with Her Ladyship."

"And Miss Cheryl has gone driving with him?" Andrina persisted.

"Yes, Miss!"

"And where is Miss Sharon?"

"She is also out, Miss."

Andrina thought it strange that neither of her sisters had told her what they were going to do before she left the house.

Lady Evelyn thought it strange too.

When they were out of ear-shot of the servants she said:

"It is naughty of the girls to behave as if I were not their Chaperon: they should have told me where they were going."

"Yes, of course, Ma'am, but as the invitations came after we had gone, I suppose they felt it would be a pity to waste such a lovely afternoon by staying indoors."

She went to her bed-room feeling more perturbed than she intended to show in front of Lady Evelyn.

Having written that letter of farewell, why then had the Marquis defied the Duke and called to see Cheryl?

She could not understand it.

Hardly realising what she was doing, she walked from her own bed-room into Cheryl's, then stood transfixed.

The place was in a turmoil. There were clothes thrown on the bed and on the chairs, a valise lay open on the floor, and the wardrobe door was left open. Then she glanced at the dressing-table.

Cheryl's brushes and combs had gone, but in the centre of the table was an envelope and it was addressed to her.

Andrina tore it open.

Dearest Andrina,

I am going away with the Marquis because he needs me. Do not let the Duke stop us. We will be married in Scotland.

Love,
Cheryl

Andrina read it, gave a little gasp, then hurried downstairs.

When she reached the Hall she said to the footman on duty:

"Is His Grace in the house?"

"No, Miss, His Grace went riding."

"Have you any idea when he will be back?"

Even to herself Andrina thought her voice sounded strange and agitated.

"His Grace did not say, Miss . . ." the footman began.

At that moment there was a sound outside the front door and when one of the flunkeys opened it Andrina saw with an inexpressible sense of relief the Duke dismounting from a black stallion.

He came up the steps looking exceedingly elegant in his polished boots and well-cut whip-cord jacket.

Andrina ran towards him.

"I must speak to you!" she said in a low voice. "Something terrible has happened!"

He looked down at the agitated and pale little face turned up to his.

Then he handed his hat, gloves, and riding-whip to one of the servants, and, taking Andrina by the arm, drew her across the Hall into the Salon.

"What has happened?" he asked.

"Cheryl has run away with the Marquis!"

As Andrina spoke she put Cheryl's note into his hand.

The Duke read it.

"Damn it!" he ejaculated angrily. "Glen had no right to do such a thing!"

"What can we do?" Andrina asked.

"Stay here!" the Duke ordered.

He walked from the room, closing the door behind him, and Andrina could hear the sound of his voice as he spoke to someone in the Hall, although she could not make out what he said.

A few moments later he came back.

"They have only been gone an hour, and as the Marquis is driving they will not have got very far. He was always ham-fisted with the ribbons!"

"We can stop them in time?" Andrina asked, her eyes suddenly alight.

"We?" the Duke questioned. "Are you coming with me?"

"Please take me," she pleaded.

He looked at her and for the moment she felt he was not sneering, not being cynical, but understanding exactly what she was feeling.

"I will take you," he said. "I have already ordered my Phaeton."

CHAPTER SIX

If Andrina had not been so agitated about Cheryl, she thought that she would have much enjoyed driving beside the Duke at a pace that was faster than she had ever been before.

She was knowledgeable enough about horse-flesh to know that he drove his four magnificent chestnuts with a remarkable expertise.

Moreover, she was aware that he looked extremely elegant with his high hat set firmly at an angle on his dark hair. His grey whip-cord coat fitted him to perfection and his boots shone brilliantly.

They had soon left behind the houses on the outskirts of London and were driving along the road northwards where there was very little traffic.

Andrina had wisely put on a small bonnet which fitted closely to her head and tied under her chin with ribbons.

As she sat back against the softly cushioned seat with a light rug over her knees, she wished that she was setting out on a happier journey than one which merely meant she must upset Cheryl by overtaking her.

How, she wondered, could the Marquis have persuaded Cheryl, who was so timid, to run away with him?

It was the last thing she would ever have expected her to do.

Cheryl was usually far too nervous to overstep the conventions or indeed to upset anyone.

"That," Andrina told herself, "is the key!"

Cheryl had not wished to be unkind to the Marquis and make him unhappy. He must have played on her feelings, assuring her that they would be married in Scotland and of course live happily ever afterwards.

The Marquis, Andrina decided, must have banked on the Duke keeping his mouth shut about his previous marriage once he and Cheryl had gone through a form of ceremony.

Andrina was quite prepared to believe that the Arkraes genuinely supposed that their son's wife was dead, and it would in fact put the Duke in a very invidious and uncomfortable position if he were to appear, after Cheryl and the Marquis had been married, to declare the ceremony null and void.

"We must catch them," Andrina told herself, "and prevent their doing anything so reprehensible!"

She wished now that she had told Cheryl the truth, but then she thought it would have been needlessly unkind for anyone, especially Lady Evelyn, who was quite obviously a gossip, to be made aware of the Marquis's secret.

They drove on and Andrina realised that the Duke was pushing his horses in a manner which she was sure was unusual for him.

Cheryl and the Marquis had an hour's start and it was imperative that they should overtake them before nightfall.

She could not believe that the Marquis, who seemed so quiet and gentlemanly, would, if they stayed at a Posting-Inn, make love to Cheryl before the ring, whether it was legitimate or not, was actually on her finger.

But apart from this aspect of the elopement, Cheryl was completely innocent and Andrina knew that she was not really in love with the Marquis.

What her reaction would be to any passionate love-making was problematical, and Andrina clasped her fingers together nervously as she thought that in all probability Cheryl would be frightened and distressed.

"Do not worry," the Duke said unexpectedly, "we shall catch them up!"

Andrina was surprised that he had sensed her agitation and she flashed him a little smile as she said:

"I am sure they are not travelling as fast as we are."

"They have only two horses," the Duke replied, "and I have yet to find a team that can outpace these."

"They are very fine."

"I have not seen you on a horse," he said, "and as it happens I have one in my stable which I think would suit you admirably."

Andrina's eyes lit up.

"I love riding, but we have never been able to afford a spirited mount."

"That is something that must be remedied," the Duke said.

Andrina did not answer.

There was no time now to think of riding when there were only a few weeks left before they would have to return home.

'If once I became accustomed to the sort of horses the Duke owns,' she thought to herself, 'it would be very hard to go back to riding poor old Dobbin, even though he has carried us all faithfully for nearly ten years!'

She kept her thoughts to herself, although she could not help imagining how exciting it would be to ride beside the Duke in the Park, or, better still, in the country, if he ever took them to Broxbourne Park.

The sun was losing its strength when, as they neared Barnet, Andrina saw ahead of them on the road a crowd of people and vehicles.

"What is it?" she asked.

"An accident!" the Duke replied briefly, and Andrina felt a sudden tremor of fear as she saw horses plunging in some disorder and a number of people scrambling out of a coach.

A second later she saw the wheel of a travelling Phaeton whirling in the air as it lay on its side, and as

the Duke began to steady down his team she saw that
a Phaeton had come into collision with a Stage-coach.

Then with a little cry of horror she saw someone in
a blue pelise being assisted from the overturned Phaeton and realised that it was Cheryl.

It was a scene of confusion, accentuated by the
plunging and rearing of the horses belonging both to
the Phaeton and the Stage-coach which was lying
drunkenly on its side in the ditch, while the passengers
were all screaming, crying, and shouting at the tops of
their voices.

The coachman, who looked as if he had recently im-
bibed too long and too deeply, was crimson in the face
as he hurled abuse at the Marquis, who, looking white
and shaken, was striving to get his horses under control.

The luggage of the passengers on the coach was
strewn about the road, some of the trunks having burst
open.

There must have been a crate of chickens being carried to London which had escaped from the coop and
were running about, clucking and getting in everybody's way.

The Duke drew his team to a standstill and as he did
so the groom, who was perched behind them, ran to
the horses' heads.

His Grace then stepped down without hurry and
lifted Andrina to the ground so that she could run to
her sister's side.

The man who had assisted Cheryl from the upturned
Phaeton had seated her on the grass and then turned
his attention elsewhere.

Cheryl appeared dazed, her bonnet had fallen back
to reveal her golden curls in untidy disorder, and there
was a scratch on her hand which was bleeding.

Andrina put her arms round her.

"Are you all right, dearest?"

"I am . . . frightened!" Cheryl replied, and burst into
tears.

Andrina held her closely.

Cheryl's gown was crumpled and her hand was bleeding, but otherwise she appeared to have suffered no particular damage and Andrina thought that it was only the shock of the accident which was making her cry.

She murmured comforting and soothing noises and found a handkerchief with which she could wipe Cheryl's eyes.

"I am . . . frightened!" she kept repeating until Andrina said briskly:

"It is all right, it is all over now. The Duke and I will take you back. You must try to forget all about it."

"I am so glad to . . . see you . . . Andrina," Cheryl said childishly.

"And I am glad to see you too, dearest."

Raising her eyes from Cheryl's unhappy face, she saw that the Duke was creating order out of chaos.

Under his instructions the male passengers and a number of spectators who had arrived at the scene of the accident were pulling the Stage-coach out of the ditch, while the horses had been calmed down and prevented from doing any damage to the shafts or their harness.

The voices of the outraged passengers seemed to die away as the Duke with an air of unquestionable authority suggested they should resume their seats so that their journey could continue.

Finally, as the Marquis seemed too bemused to do anything sensible, the Duke tipped the coachman so as to put him in a good humour.

Almost before it seemed possible the trunks were stowed back on the roof, the chickens were collected and returned to their coop, and the Stage-coach set off again towards London.

The same willing spectators righted the Phaeton in which the Marquis and Cheryl had been travelling, but it was obvious that one of the wheels was buckled and it could not proceed far without attention.

"You had better take it to Barnet," the Duke said to

the Marquis. "There will be a wheelwright there, and doubtless you can hire a post-chaise."

The Marquis did not reply.

Instead he looked to where Cheryl was seated on the grass beside Andrina.

"I will take Cheryl back with me," the Duke said quietly.

The eyes of the two men met and just for one second it seemed as if the Marquis might defy the Duke. Then with his habitual look of indecision his eyes flickered and he replied:

"Perhaps that would be—best."

"I am sure it is."

The Duke walked away without saying any more and getting into his own Phaeton turned the horses with some considerable skill on the narrow road and drew them up beside Andrina and Cheryl.

Cheryl allowed her sister to help her into the Duke's Phaeton without, it seemed, sparing a thought for the unhappy Marquis. He stood watching them depart, without however making any effort to approach her.

The Phaeton, which had been designed for two people, was fortunately wide enough for three, especially as Andrina and Cheryl were both so slim.

Andrina seated Cheryl between herself and the Duke and put her arms round her sister's shoulders.

They drove off without anyone speaking and only when they had gone for perhaps a mile did Cheryl say:

"I am . . . sorry, Andrina!"

"Why did you do it, dearest?"

"He said he would be so . . . unhappy without me," Cheryl answered, "and I h-hate people being . . . unhappy."

That was true enough, Andrina thought, and it was a very sweet part of Cheryl's nature. But she could not help wondering how her sister, could go through life without disastrous results, doing everything she was asked to do.

It was difficult, however, to have an intimate conversation as the Duke was driving very fast and there was an evening breeze which seemed to whip the words away from their lips.

Andrina therefore contented herself with holding Cheryl comfortably in her arms and feeling grateful that she had arrived there so soon after the accident.

She wondered whether, if they had not reached them in time, Cheryl would have demanded to be taken home.

She had a feeling that she would have done so, and that would have been no less embarrassing to the Marquis than what had happened now.

Anyway it was all very upsetting, and Andrina could only hope that Cheryl would not now take a dislike to every man she met and perhaps even refuse to go to parties.

She had always been absurdly sensitive when anything went wrong, and all through her life Andrina could remember Cheryl being depressed and unhappy about the smallest slight or the faintest criticism.

She realised that at the moment her sister was still in a daze and she could not help feeling a little apprehensive about what would happen once they reached Broxbourne House.

There was however nothing she could do but hope that both Lady Evelyn and Sharon would be tactful, and she was determined that she would protect Cheryl in every possible way.

It was nearly seven o'clock when they turned into Curzon Street and Andrina wondered whether anyone had had the sense to let the Princess de Lieven know that they would be late for dinner.

It was quite obvious that Cheryl would not wish to go, and she wondered how she could explain that she must stay with her sister without making anyone suspicious as to what Cheryl's indiscretion might have been.

The Duke drew the horses to a standstill and footmen hurried forward to help first Andrina and then Cheryl down from the carriage.

They walked up the steps side by side. Then as they

entered the Hall, Andrina saw that there was a man
standing at the far end of it.

She had only given him a casual glance before
Cheryl uttered a loud cry and ran across the marble
floor with her arms outstretched.

"Hugo! Hugo!" she exclaimed.

It was Hugo Renton and Andrina was surprised to
see him, but before she could even move Cheryl had
flung her arms round him, saying:

"I am so glad you are here! You said I would not
like it, and you were right! I want to go home!"

Hugo Renton looked down at her lovely face and his
arms went round her.

"That is just what I have come to suggest, my darling," he answered. "My father is dead and now we
can be married!"

"Oh, Hugo! Hugo!"

With a cry of sheer happiness Cheryl put her arms
round Hugo's neck and he was holding her closely to
him, quite oblivious of Andrina, standing still, unable
to move, and of the flunkeys staring with undisguised
curiosity.

"No! No!" Andrina said almost beneath her breath.

Then as she would have gone towards her sister she
felt the Duke's restraining hand on her arm.

He walked towards Cheryl and Hugo Renton, and as
he reached their side Cheryl looked up at him, her blue
eyes swimming with tears but with a radiance on her
face that made her lovelier than she had ever been before.

"This is Hugo, Your Grace!" she said, as if she felt
an explanation was necessary.

"So I gather!" the Duke answered. "Shall we go
somewhere a little more private where we can discuss
his arrival?"

"Of course," Cheryl agreed happily.

She took her arms reluctantly from Hugo Renton's
neck and he looked at the Duke in a somewhat embarrassed manner, then held out his hand.

"I must apologise, Your Grace."

"It is quite unnecessary," the Duke replied.

He made a gesture indicating the Salon and the footmen opened the doors.

They walked inside, Andrina feeling that there was a great deal she ought to say but having no idea how to say it.

There was no doubt, she thought, as she walked behind Cheryl and Hugo Renton, who were following the Duke towards the fireplace, that Hugo was a very different sort of man from the Marquis.

He too was quiet and gentle, but he also had a determination and a strength about him which the Marquis had never shown.

Andrina was aware that he had loved Cheryl ever since they were children, but she had never thought he was good enough for Cheryl as a husband simply because she had always had such ambitious schemes for her two beautiful sisters.

The Rentons were a well-known County family who owned a comfortable house surrounded by a small Estate, but she had wanted something more than that for Cheryl.

Yet, looking at her sister now, her fear and unhappiness swept away as if my magic, it was impossible not to know that it was Hugo she loved, if she was capable of loving anyone very deeply.

"I knew this was where Cheryl and her sisters were staying, Your Grace," Hugo Renton was saying, "and since I arrived I have learnt from Sharon that you are their Guardian."

"That is correct!" the Duke agreed. "And as far as I am concerned, if Cheryl wishes to become your wife, she has both my permission and my blessing!"

Cheryl gave another cry of delight and put her arms round Hugo again.

"I am very grateful to Your Grace," Hugo Renton said.

Then he looked down at Cheryl's lovely face and it was obvious he could think of nothing else.

The Duke turned to Andrina with a twist of his lips.

"I think you and I are slightly *de trop* at this moment."

Andrina drew a deep breath.

She wanted to protest, she wanted to say this was not what she had envisaged or planned for Cheryl, but she knew it was useless.

Cheryl had made her choice. It was obvious from the way she was clinging to Hugo and the happiness in her face that it would be cruel even to suggest that she should look elsewhere.

Philosophically Andrina shrugged her shoulders and as she acquiesced to the Duke's suggestion and turned to walk towards the door, she saw a twinkle in his eye.

He knew full well that her ambitions for her sister had been dashed and she was in fact bitterly disappointed.

"He is pleased to see me discomfited," she told herself.

Because she would not give him the satisfaction of seeing that she was upset, she lifted her chin a little higher and gave him a defiant glance as they walked towards the door.

They had almost reached it when it opened and two people came into the room.

It was Sharon, already dressed for dinner and looking extremely lovely, accompanied by the Count, who appeared more handsome and elegant than usual, with an exquisitely tied cravat, a frilled shirt, and a coat of dark blue satin.

"You are going to be very late . . ." Sharon began.

Then she looked to the other end of the room and saw Hugo and Cheryl with their arms round each other.

"What is . . . happening?" she began. "Why, it is Hugo!"

"An old friend," the Duke remarked laconically. "You must congratulate your sister. She has found, without any effort on our part, the man she wishes to marry!"

"And so have I!" Sharon exclaimed.

Then as Andrina stiffened, Sharon realised that she had spoken impetuously and the colour rose in her face.

Her eyes turned towards the Count as he said quickly to the Duke:

"I intended to speak to Your Grace at the first available opportunity."

There was a smile on the Duke's lips as he said drily:

"It seems usual in this family for everyone to make their arrangements first and ask afterwards!"

"Are you saying, Sharon, that you wish to marry the Count?" Andrina asked in a voice that shook.

Sharon gave her sister a brilliant smile.

"I intend to marry him!" she answered. "Oh, Andrina, I am so happy! Do not say anything to spoil it!"

She bent forward to kiss her sister as she spoke and there was so much excitement in her voice that Andrina found her protests dying away even before they were spoken.

It would have been as impossible to do anything to dim the radiance in Sharon's face as it had been in Cheryl's case, and now she ran across the room to kiss her younger sister and tell her the news.

"I think this calls for a celebration!" the Duke remarked.

He ordered the Butler to bring champagne, then looked at Andrina, who was watching her sisters chattering to each other at the other end of the room while the Count and Hugo were introducing themselves to each other.

"They are both very happy," the Duke said quietly.

Andrina started because she had not realised that he was so close beside her.

"They are not the marriages I had hoped for," she replied.

Then because she felt that he might be gloating over her discomfiture, she turned and walked from the room and upstairs to her bed-room.

Her maid was waiting to help her into a very elaborate Ball-gown, but she shook her head.

"I shall not be going out this evening," she said. "Will you inform Lady Evelyn that I shall stay behind with Miss Cheryl, who, I am certain, will not wish to go to the Russian Embassy."

Even as she was speaking Lady Evelyn came into the room.

"I understand you have brought Cheryl back," she said.

"She is here," Andrina answered, "and she is engaged to Hugo Renton—a man she has known ever since she was a child!"

"Oh, I am glad!" Lady Evelyn exclaimed.

Andrina looked at her in surprise.

"Cheryl confided to me that there was a man she liked more than any other she had met," Lady Evelyn explained, "and Sharon told me all about him."

She could see the disappointment in Andrina's eyes and she said quietly:

"My dear, Cheryl is very beautiful, but as you well know, she would never cope with the difficulties and intrigues of the Social world. She needs someone to look after her and make decisions for her. She will be perfectly happy in the country with a husband and their babies. She is not cut out for anything else."

"She is so beautiful!" Andrina murmured.

Then she added in a sharp voice:

"Sharon is to marry the Count. Did you know that?"

"They told me when they came back from their drive," Lady Evelyn replied. "I consider them very suitably matched."

"He is poor and of no importance," Andrina protested.

"He is ambitious and very clever!" Lady Evelyn answered. "What he needs is a wife who will adore him, and at the same time do everything to further his career. It will keep Sharon busy and I am quite certain that after a great deal of hard work they will achieve success."

"I suppose you think I am very mercenary," Andrina said.

"I think that like all match-making women you are blinded by the golden glitter of the *Beau Monde* and do not see the heart-break that often lies beneath it," Lady Evelyn answered.

She glanced at the clock on the mantelpiece and gave a little cry.

"We must go! The Princess will never forgive us if we are late. The Count said he would call for us and I imagine that he and Sharon are downstairs. What about you and Cheryl?"

"I am quite certain Cheryl will want to stay here with Hugo," Andrina replied, "and, as they must be Chaperoned, I will stay with them."

"Very well," Lady Evelyn said, "but do not be too arduous in your duties. A good Chaperon should know when to make herself scarce!"

*   *   *

The Duke also stayed at home instead of attending the party at the Russian Embassy.

They had dinner in the large and formal Dining-Room, but Andrina could not help thinking it was the gayest meal she had eaten since she had been at Broxbourne House.

Cheryl was so happy that it seemed to shine from her like a light, and Hugo, who Andrina had always thought was rather heavy and dull, seemed to have developed the art of conversation, which she had never noticed in the past.

Granted, he talked of horses and country affairs, but the Duke was obviously knowledgeable on both subjects and Andrina found herself being much more amused by their present conversation than by the social gossip she had listened to on other nights.

When dinner was over the Duke said he was going to his Club, and remembering that Lady Evelyn had told her not to be too arduous a Chaperon, Andrina left Cheryl and Hugo alone in the Salon and went, somewhat forlornly, up the stairs to her bed-room.

When she reached it the maid who was waiting to undo her gown brought her two jewel-boxes.

"Miss Cheryl was going to wear these tonight at the Ball, Miss," she said, "but as she changed in a hurry she didn't put them on. I wonder if you'd like me to take them down to Mr. Robson?"

"I will take them," Andrina said. "Will he be up at this hour of the night?"

"Oh, yes, Miss, he usually works late and anyway he has his private rooms just the other side of the office."

"I will take them to him," Andrina said.

She went downstairs again and along the passage to Mr. Robson's office.

She opened the door to find him sitting at his desk, dealing with a number of papers.

He looked up in surprise as she entered.

"I am returning some jewellery," Andrina explained. "My sister has not gone to the Russian Embassy and so she does not require it."

"It is very kind of you, Miss Andrina," Mr. Robson said, rising to his feet, "but it could easily have waited until the morning when, I hope, Miss Sharon brings me back the diamond stars in safety."

"I noticed she had them in her hair," Andrina said.

"She told me it was a very special evening for her," Mr. Robson replied, and he was smiling.

"I suppose it is," Andrina agreed. "Both my sisters have become engaged!"

"Then it is indeed very, very special!"

He carried the jewel-boxes across the room and opened the safe-door.

Andrina looked down on the desk at which he had been working, by the light of a candelabrum which held three candles.

She could not help seeing what was written in large letters on a folder which lay in the centre of the desk.

Charities supported anonymously by
His Grace, the Duke of Broxbourne.

For a moment Andrina stared at the words. Then in curiosity, without realising that she was prying, she opened the outside cover of the folder.

On the next page in Mr. Robson's meticulous copper-plate hand-writing there was a list:

1) *Orphanages and orphans*
2) *Pensioners*
3) *Reformed Criminals*
4) *First Offenders*
5) *Society for the Abolition of Climbing Boys*
6) *Foster-Parents for Illegitimate and Ill-treated Children*
7) *The Blind*
8) *The Anti-Slavery Movement*
9) *Abolition of Children's labour in the factories and mines*
10) *Society for Prevention of Cruelty to Animals*

Andrina read it, her eyes wide with surprise. Then she heard Mr. Robson make an exclamation as he came from the safe and realised what she had been doing.

"That is not for your eyes, Miss Andrina!"

"Why not?" Andrina enquired.

"Because," Mr. Robson replied, "the Duke would be extremely annoyed if he knew you had seen it."

"But why?"

"Because His Grace does not wish anyone to know of his kindness in so many different ways."

Andrina deliberately picked up the folder and opened it. It was very thick, and as she turned the pages she could see dozens and dozens of names, and against each one the dates on which they had received considerable sums of money.

"Why should the Duke wish to be so secretive about this?" she asked.

Mr. Robson seemed to hesitate and she said:

"I would like to know the truth. Of course, I could ask him myself."

"I hope you will not do that, Miss Andrina," Mr. Robson said hastily. "His Grace would be extremely incensed with me if he knew you had seen this folder. He has impressed upon me often enough that it must be kept under lock and key."

He paused to add:

"You surprised me by coming here this evening, and therefore as you might say I was off my guard."

"I will keep your secret and the Duke's," Andrina said, "if you will explain to me why His Grace should not want anyone to know he is so generous."

As she spoke she sat down on Mr. Robson's chair at his desk, still holding the folder in her hands.

She knew he was debating within himself whether he should trust her with the truth. Finally he made up his mind and began:

"I suppose, as you are a relation, Miss Andrina, there will be no harm in my telling you what you want to know, even though His Grace would be very angry if he learnt about it."

"Go on, Mr. Robson!" Andrina prompted.

"I have been in the service of Duke and of his father before him for nearly fifty years," Mr. Robson said, "and so I have been privileged perhaps to see more of the family even than those who are closer through a blood relationship."

Andrina's eyes were on his face as he went on:

"The old Duke was always a difficult man, and when he lost the Duchess, all that was kind and pleasant in his nature vanished overnight! He became soured, and I think he hated everybody, but most of all he hated his only child!"

"The present Duke?"

"His Grace!" Mr. Robson agreed. "He was only a little boy of six when his mother died, and from that moment everything that was gentle and loving in his life was taken from him."

"How was that?" Andrina enquired.

"As I have said, the old Duke hated the young Marquis, as he was then. He never spoke to him except unkindly, harshly, and to find fault, and he took away from him everything and everybody of whom he was fond."

There was a note of pain in Mr. Robson's voice that told Andrina that he had hated to stand by and see the child suffer.

"If Master Tancred, as we called him, became fond of a Nurse or a Governess, she was dismissed," Mr. Robson continued. "He cried bitterly when his Nurse was sent away and he cried two years later when Miss Anstruther, a nice, kind woman, was told to go."

"But why did the old Duke get rid of them?" Andrina enquired.

"I think because he suffered himself he wanted his son to suffer too," Mr. Robson replied. "Anyway, it was terrible for us who cared for the little boy to see the manner in which he was being persecuted."

He gave a deep sigh before he went on:

"When the young Marquis grew older, if he took a liking to a horse, his father sold it. He had a sporting-dog once to which he became very attached and the Duke ordered it to be shot!"

"Oh, no!" Andrina cried. "I cannot bear it!"

"That is what we used to say, Miss Andrina," Mr. Robson said, "but there was nothing we could do and we did not dare even express our sympathy to His Lordship."

"Why not?" Andrina enquired.

"Because he was very proud. Even when he was young he had a pride which made him hide his feelings. I knew that he missed his mother desperately and after her the two women of whom he had grown fond. But when he lost them, he was determined not to let anyone, least of all his father, know that he cared."

"So that was why he grew so cynical," Andrina said almost to herself.

"That is why His Grace put up a defence between himself and the world," Mr. Robson said. "He would not be pitied. He would not allow anyone to feel sorry for him, and so he wanted them to believe that nothing they could do or say could possibly hurt him in any way."

Andrina drew a deep breath.

Now she could understand so much that had puzzled her before. Now she could see why the Duke appeared indifferent to everyone's feelings except his own, why he had an imperious aloofness which had made him seem to her to be autocratic and tyrannical.

"He must have been very unhappy," she said softly at length.

"I used to lie awake at nights," Mr. Robson said, "worrying over him; but even before His Grace went to Eton we none of us dared show him how sorry we were for him."

There was a sad note in Mr. Robson's voice.

"I think as he grew older, knowing how unapproachable, how difficult, and how feared the old Duke was, he has modelled himself on his father. But beneath it all His Grace has a kind heart and a sympathy with those who are unfortunate. It is only that he is determined not to let anyone know it!"

"So he helps all these people secretly," Andrina said, looking at the folder which was still in her hands.

"He has threatened to dismiss me, after all these years, if I ever speak of it outside this room," Mr. Robson said, with a smile. "That is why my future is in your hands, Miss Andrina."

"I will not betray you," she promised. "At the same time, I am glad to know the truth. I could not understand how His Grace could be so cynical, why there seemed to be nothing but hardness about him."

"It would have been very different had the Duchess, his mother, lived," Mr. Robson said. "She was always lovely and gentle. Everyone she knew adored her. I suppose we could all understand what the old Duke felt when she died, but it would have broken her heart to see Master Tancred made to suffer the way he did."

Andrina put the folder down on the desk.

"Thank you for telling me."

"And you will not give me away, Miss Andrina?" Mr. Robson asked anxiously.

"You have my word of honour on that."

Andrina went up to her bed-room and when she was in bed she thought she would be tired and sleepy after all she had been through that day.

Instead she found herself thinking of the Duke, but not as she knew him, raging at her for her behaviour, making her feel insignificant, embarrassed, and angry.

Rather, she thought of the Duke Mr. Robson had described to her! The unhappy little boy who had lost his mother and who cried at night because she was not there, the child whose Nurse was taken away because he was too fond of her, and whose Governess was dismissed for the same reason.

She could hardly bear to think how he must have suffered when his dog was destroyed by a tyrannical, cruel father who must have been half mad, and yet in his own way was suffering unbearably over the loss of the woman he loved.

Andrina found that it hurt her physically to think of so much unhappiness which had turned from the solace of tears to a hardness which had become a cynicism worn as an armour and a defence against being hurt again.

'That is the real secret,' she thought.

The Duke had suffered so much that he would not allow himself to suffer anymore. That was why he had fought against his generous impulse in taking them into his house, why he showed them no other feelings save indifference and reserve.

It was almost as if, Andrina thought, he had positively wanted her to hate him, and therefore had gone out of his way to provoke, to mock her, and almost to delight in finding her in the wrong.

It was all part of the aggression which had sprung from unhappiness too deep and too painful for him to contemplate it, and yet which remained inside him whatever he did, however much he tried to escape it.

"Perhaps someday he will find happiness," Andrina told herself.

She thought of the expression in Hugo Renton's eyes as he looked down at Cheryl and the note in his voice when he had said that he wanted to marry her.

There was a depth and sincerity expressing an emotion which seemed to come from the very depth of his being.

And what she had seen in Hugo she had also seen in the Count. He and Sharon must have loved each other from the first moment they met.

Andrina had told the Earl of Crowhurst that love at first sight only happened in novels, but it had certainly happened to Sharon and Count Ivan! And she knew that Lady Evelyn was right when she said that they would be successful because they were so much in love.

"I suppose," Andrina said to herself, "that is what we all want: a love that makes a woman shine with delight and a man have a depth and a wonder in his voice because of what he feels within his heart."

"Perhaps one day," she went on, almost as if she were telling herself a story, "a little boy called Tancred, whose love has always been taken from him, will find it again."

It would change him, she thought, so that he would no longer fight the world and everyone in it. He would no longer want people to think him selfish and egotistical, he would no longer feel afraid of his own kind impulses.

Only love, the love that he had lost when he was very small, could bring him that.

Then as once again her thoughts shied away from the horror of what he must have felt when his dog had been destroyed, she knew how much she wanted his happiness.

She had hated him, and she told herself firmly she still did; yet she wanted to make up to him for all those wasted years when in his father's eyes he could do nothing right and he had no-one to turn to.

It was strange, she thought, how thinking about his sufferings really hurt her.

It was almost as if someone had turned a knife in her heart, and she wondered if, when she saw the Duke again, she would ever be able to storm and rage at him as she had done before.

She would certainly no longer be able to look at him with the same eyes, no longer see a man deliberately provoking her, insulting her, and criticising her, but instead only a lonely, pathetic, unhappy little boy.

"This is ridiculous!" Andrina said aloud. "I must go to sleep. There is so much to be done tomorrow, and I must think about a trousseau for Cheryl and for Sharon. Why am I lying here worrying over the Duke?"

She turned over, patted her pillow, and settled herself down again, and yet the pain in her heart was still there.

Strangely she felt curiously like tears—tears for something that had happened a long, long time ago.

"Someone will make it up to him one day," she told herself consolingly.

Then almost as if a voice beside her spoke, there was the question:

"Why not you?"

Andrina sat bolt upright in bed.

For a moment she could hardly imagine what she was doing or thinking. Then she suddenly knew that her thoughts and her feelings had been carrying her along a path that had been there long before she had talked to Mr. Robson.

Whatever she might tell herself to the contrary, it had been fascinating to talk to the Duke, to fight him, to argue with him, and even, strangely enough, to be defeated by him.

He made her very angry, and yet she admitted to herself now that when he was not there a room seemed empty and a party dull.

It was not only being beside him; there was some

strange attraction she had never dared admit to herself
in seeing him looking so distinguished, and yet so indifferent.

She knew now that she had been tinglingly aware of
him from the moment she woke up in the morning in
his house to the moment she went to bed.

She had refused to admit it, and yet when she had
dressed she had taken extra pains to look her best just
because she might see him.

Again, although she kept it a secret even from her
own thoughts, she had known that her heart seemed to
turn over in her breast and beat a little faster the moment he appeared.

And yet she had managed to tell herself that he was
everything that was despicable, a man who cared for
no-one but himself, and she had it on Lady Evelyn's
authority that he was as selfish and ungenerous as his
father.

Rich though he was, he would not even offer anyone
hospitality unless it was for his own particular amusement.

Now she had seen with her own eyes the manner in
which he cared for so many less-fortunate people, and
she had learnt the reason for his cynicism. His air of
superiority was not at all what she had supposed, but
just a fear of being hurt even more than he had been
already.

Was it surprising, when he had such a fine nature
hidden away, that he had despised her from the very
moment they had met?

He thought of her first as an immoral woman; then
because she had somehow forced him into the position
of introducing them to Society, unwillingly and unchar-
acteristically, he must have hated her as she hated him.

Then he despised her for the manner in which she
had behaved with Lord Crowhurst and because he had
seen her as she was, a snob and a social climber where
her sisters were concerned.

She could imagine how such low standards and

frivolous values would disgust him, and she could understand too how while he gladly helped people who were really poor and suffering, he must have loathed her for her pretensions.

At that moment Andrina went down into a little hell of her own, in which she faced herself and was horrified by what she found.

'I wanted all the wrong things,' she thought miserably, 'titles, money, position. I forgot that the only thing that really matters is what the Duke has never had—love!'

She saw herself scrabbling, clawing, and fighting to make Cheryl a Duchess, when all Cheryl wanted was to be safe in Hugo's arms.

She saw herself doing the same with Sharon, who had been clever enough to find the Count without her assistance.

"I was wrong right from the beginning," Andrina admitted to herself humbly. "I aimed for the wrong things and wanted nothing that was really worth having."

Every woman wanted a husband, she thought, but only with love. All the rest was of no possible consequence.

"No-one will ever love me," Andrina told herself miserably, "not in the way I want to be loved."

She realised as she thought about it that beauty could be just as transient and as insubstantial in regard to happiness as a title and a great position.

It blinded those who looked at it to the real person who lay beneath.

A beautiful face without a heart and a soul that matched it was as undesirable as marrying a title without love.

"How could I have been such a fool?" Andrina asked herself, and remembered that the Duke had called her "foolish" not once but many times.

He was right, she thought, and threw herself back against the pillows to hide her face.

"He was right and I was wrong" she whispered, "and, oh, God . . . I cannot think how it has . . . happened . . . but I love him!"

CHAPTER SEVEN

The two married couples drove away amidst a shower of rice and rose-petals.

There was a cheer from the male members of the party as the carriages moved down the short drive into Curzon Street; then, laughing and talking, everyone began to disperse.

It had been intended that the wedding should be very quiet, and it was in fact Hugo Renton who had suggested that it should take place as quickly as possible.

"I am in mourning," he said, "and since there is a great deal for me to do following my father's death, I must return to the country."

He looked at Andrina and added:

"But I do not wish to leave Cheryl behind."

Andrina had not spoken and he went on:

"She will be worried and indecisive if she is not with me. Besides, I have suffered enough, thinking of her here in London and that she might forget all about me."

"I understand," Andrina said and meant it.

She would not have been able to understand a week earlier, but now her own feelings for the Duke made her tender and compassionate towards both her sisters.

She could realise so well what they were feeling and surprisingly it was the Duke who made everything easy.

"You had best both be married at the same time," he said. "Ivan tells me that he can obtain a short leave

149

of absence from his Embassy and he naturally wishes to spend it on his honeymoon.

"If either of you has a long engagement, the Season will be over and then, if you wish any of your friends or relatives to be present, it will be the autumn before anyone is back in London again."

Andrina could not help wondering whether this explanation, which sounded so logical, arose from genuine solicitude for Cheryl's and Sharon's happiness, or if the Duke was in fact longing to be rid of them all and to have his house to himself again.

Naturally the two couples concerned agreed fervently with everything the Duke suggested, and in an incredibly short space of time the marriage was arranged and everything was planned.

They thought at first that practically no-one should be invited except their immediate relatives, but however hard they tried, there always seemed to be some very viable excuse why someone extra should be included.

First it was obvious that the Russian Ambassador and the Princess de Lieven must be present, then Hugo felt obliged to ask not only his sisters and his grandmother, who was still living, but a large number of cousins.

That alone would not have swelled the congregation unduly, until they started to total up the number of Broxbourne relatives, and Lady Evelyn averred that they would never speak to Cheryl or Sharon if they were left out.

And so in the end St. George's, Hanover Square, was filled to capacity and the Ball-Room at Broxbourne House was once again opened for the Reception.

There was a luncheon-party which was indeed confined to the more immediate relatives, but after everyone returned from the Church there was champagne, a buffet loaded with delicacies, and two wedding-cakes made by the Duke's Chef, which were nearly six feet high.

Andrina had been thankful that Mr. Robson saw to

all the innumerable details of the wedding, including
the listing of the presents, and all she had to do was to
buy what was necessary for Cheryl's and Sharon's
trousseaux.

That was enough in itself!

As she said to Lady Evelyn over and over again:

"Surely they cannot need so many clothes? They will
be out of fashion long before they have worn them!"

But because she loved her sisters she did not protest unduly, even though she kept worrying as to how
everything would be paid for and felt extremely guilty
about the debts she was certain she was incurring in
the Duke's name.

She hoped she would have an opportunity to talk
with him about it, but the days before the wedding
swept by with a thousand things for her to do.

Cheryl and Sharon were continually asking her ad-
vice or assistance and Lady Evelyn was prepared to
leave everything in her hands, so that when she went to
bed at night she fell asleep almost immediately from
sheer exhaustion.

Yet it was a delight and a comfort to know that the
Duke was there.

Sometimes she had only a glimpse of him riding away
from the front door on his black stallion; sometimes he
joined them for a short time before dinner, when he
usually seemed to have engagements which were different from their own.

She wondered if he was bored with their company or
if he was being tactful and wished to leave the young
couples to their own devices.

It was quite obvious that neither Cheryl and Hugo
nor Sharon and Count Ivan needed anyone but each
other.

Andrina could not help feeling lonely and left out of
things.

She was so used to having her sisters cling to her
and to being the centre of their small world that it was
difficult not to feel a little jealous when she found her-

self almost forgotten in their preoccupation with the men they loved.

Because she was so busy she gave little thought to her own future after Cheryl and Sharon were married.

Sometimes it seemed to her a little strange that she had no admirers and that the men who said flattering and complimentary things at parties never seemed to make any further effort, such as calling at Broxbourne House, or even sending her flowers.

But she was too thankful not to have to cope with Lord Crowhurst for it to worry her unduly.

She saw him occasionally in the distance, but he made no attempt to approach her and she knew that the Duke had dealt very effectively with him and he would trouble her no longer.

Then she asked herself if she could be sure of that.

After all, when she was no longer under the Duke's protection, when she had returned home and was alone at the Manor House, it would be quite possible for Lord Crowhurst to force himself upon her if he still wished to do so, and there would be no-one to whom she could turn for help.

She tried to dismiss the thought but it was there at the back of her mind, and sometimes she would awaken in the middle of the night and feel afraid.

And yet she was very happy for her sisters as she followed them up the aisle.

They walked ahead of her, one on each arm of the Duke, both looking so beautiful that it seemed to Andrina as if the whole congregation drew in a deep breath at the sight of them.

Cheryl was wearing white. The gossamer-net gown which Andrina had bought her as a present had been ornamented with tiny bunches of orange-blossom.

The veil over her lovely face and golden hair, the bouquet of roses and lily-of-the-valley, made her the embodiment of everything one could imagine a youthful bride should be.

Sharon, in gold lamé, looked like a Persian Princess. With a diamond tiara glittering on her head and a bouquet of exotic orchids, she was a picture of mystery and allure.

And no-one, Andrina decided, could look more distinguished or more handsome than the Duke.

His hair was brushed in the wind-swept style that had been made fashionable by the Prince Regent. He wore a diamond decoration on his coat, and his tall, athletic figure moving between the two beautiful brides made a picture it would be difficult for anyone present in the Church ever to forget.

The voices of the choir, the scent of the lilies, and the beautiful words of the Marriage-Service moved Andrina almost to tears.

Then as Cheryl and Sharon came down the aisle on the arms of their husbands, she felt as if besides the glittering, distinguished congregation there was a cloud of angels somewhere singing a hymn of praise.

"I am so happy! So very, very happy, Andrina!" Cheryl cried as, having changed into her going-away gown, she kissed her sister good-bye.

"I am glad, darling," Andrina replied. "Hugo will look after you and I shall be seeing you very soon."

"I expect you will be coming to the Manor," Cheryl said. "That will be fun!"

"Yes, it will," Andrina agreed.

Sharon, however, had something very different to say.

Andrina went to her room to find her putting the last touches to her going-away outfit of emerald green, which suited her better than anything she had ever worn.

"What are you going to do, Andrina?" she asked, looking at her sister's reflection behind her in the mirror.

"Tidy up, I expect!" Andrina replied with a smile.

"I mean after that," Sharon said. "You will not be able to stay here for long. Lady Evelyn is talking of going to France. She has been asked to stay with our Ambassador in Paris and she is very excited about it."

"I expect I shall go home," Andrina said.

"I see we have been very selfish," Sharon remarked suddenly. "Cheryl and I have been so busy getting married we have forgotten about you! As you are the oldest, you should have been married first."

"I expect I shall be an old maid," Andrina smiled.

"I am prepared to wager that that will not happen!" Sharon answered. "Hurry up and find a husband, Andrina. It is wonderful being in love!"

Her voice softened and her eyes were shining as she thought of Ivan. Then, as if she could not bear to be apart from him any longer, she said:

"I must go! Thank you, Andrina, darling, for everything! I should never have met Ivan but for you, and I can never be grateful enough!"

"Take care of yourself, dearest," Andrina said, but Sharon was already out of ear-shot, running down the stairs as if she was afraid Ivan might leave without her.

Both the girls thanked the Duke very prettily, Cheryl a little shyly, but Sharon put her arms round his neck and pulled his head down to hers.

"Thank you!" she said, kissing his cheek. "You have been the most perfect Guardian. No-one could have been kinder!"

It gave Andrina a strange feeling in her breast to see Sharon kissing the Duke.

Once—it seemed a long time ago now—she had thought that her sister might become the Duchess of Broxbourne, but now she knew it would have been an agony beyond words to see the Duke, to be near him, and know that he was her brother-in-law.

'Better not to see him at all,' she thought to herself, 'than to be tortured by pangs of jealousy which would have been shaming but which I would have been unable to suppress.'

Gradually the last and most reluctant of the guests left the house.

They took with them Lady Evelyn, who had promised to dine with some relatives who had come up to London for the wedding and who were leaving early the following morning.

"You will be all right, Andrina?" she asked casually as she moved towards the front door.

"Yes, of course," Andrina replied.

She could not however help feeling that everything had gone depressingly flat. Then as she stood irresolutely wondering what she should do, she heard the Duke's voice behind her saying:

"I wish to speak to you, Andrina. Shall we go into the Library?"

It was the only room in the house on which the wedding had been allowed to make no impact.

The other rooms were filled with wedding-presents and a preponderance of white flowers, or else littered with empty glasses and plates of food which the servants were just beginning to remove.

The Library looked just as it always did and somehow it seemed to Andrina to bring them back to the commonplace.

It made her realise that now that the excitement was over she had to make plans for the future and be practical about herself.

She walked across the room slowly, knowing that the Duke was looking at her.

She wondered if he realised she was wearing the same pink gown she had worn the night he had raged at her in the garden after Lord Crowhurst had attempted to kiss her in the arbour.

It had seemed a quite unnecessary expense, when she had only worn the gown once, to buy a new one. And it had been skilfully altered by Madame Bertin so that it was exactly what she needed as bride's-maid.

She was even wearing the same wreath on her head which the Duke had told her to straighten, and once again she had refused to ornament herself with any of the Broxbourne jewellry, having no wish to compete with Sharon's glittering appearance.

"Come and sit down,' the Duke suggested. "Would you like a glass of wine or something to eat?"

Andrina shook her head.

"We seem to have eaten and drunk so much already today."

"I want to talk to you, Andrina!"

"What about?" she asked nervously.

"Yourself! I am interested to know your plans for the future."

"Cheryl asked me the same thing. I suppose I will go home."

"Home?"

"There is no-one to go with me . . . but our old maid Sarah will be there."

"And you consider that an adequate protection?"

Andrina thought of the Earl of Crowhurst and hesitated. Then she put up her chin.

"I will manage, Your Grace."

"I find this is not very reassuring, considering your experiences in the past."

Andrina was silent. Then, anxious to change the subject, she said:

"I want to speak with Your Grace on another matter."

"What is that?" he enquired.

"Now that the wedding is over, I have to know how much I owe you."

The Duke did not reply and she went on:

"I am not so mutton-headed as not to realise that we must have spent much more than the original five hundred pounds that you obtained for the necklace. So I must insist on Your Grace telling me the truth and letting me know how deeply I stand in your debt."

"Most women are very content to have their bills paid for them," the Duke said.

"Then I must be different from most women of Your Grace's acquaintance," Andrina replied. "I wish for no favours."

"Very well!"

The Duke walked to his desk as he spoke and drew a piece of paper from one of the drawers.

He handed it to Andrina. She expected it to be a

summary of the bills from the dress-makers which had all been sent to him.

Instead, she saw it was headed with the name Hunt and Roskell, a well-known Court Jeweller. Beneath was written:

> *On Your Grace's instructions we have valued the necklace of Indian design. We would respectfully point out that while this is an interesting piece of native work and would undoubtedly be prized by collectors, it is in fact of little intrinsic value. The rubies and pearls are real, but of inferior quality, the emeralds are false. It is therefore our opinion that the necklace in a Sale-room might fetch the sum of perhaps forty or fifty pounds.*
>
> *We remain Your Grace's most respectful and humble servants,*
>
> *Hunt and Roskell*

Andrina read the letter and gave a little gasp.

"It cannot be true!"

Even as she spoke she knew that it was typical of her father to have brought back from India something spectacular which had interested and intrigued him without taking the trouble to find out its true value.

"I must owe you a great deal of . . . money," she gasped after a moment.

"A considerable sum!" the Duke agreed.

She felt that in his own peculiar way he was pleased at her dismay, and because her pride would not let her be down-trodden she said:

"I will pay you back . . . that I promise you, but it will take a . . . long time."

"A life-time!" the Duke remarked.

"Perhaps not as . . . long as that," Andrina said, "but certainly . . . many years."

Even as she was speaking she was thinking that without the girls to care for, if she was really thrifty and spent practically nothing at all on herself, she might be able to repay him a hundred pounds a year out of her tiny income.

But the idea of a debt stretching on and on into the future was terrifying and made her feel as though she were entering a long tunnel and there was no light at the end of it.

She was staring blindly at the letter from the jewellers and after a moment the Duke said:

"I think by this time, Andrina, you know that I seldom give something for nothing, and I expect you to make good any expenditure I have made on your behalf."

"I will . . . pay you . . . back, in time," Andrina said.

She was still calculating wildly how long it would take her and thinking that perhaps the Duke was right: she would be dead long before she was finally clear of her debt!

"I prefer to be paid at once!"

She raised her head to look at him, her eyes wide and worried, her face very pale with the shock of what he had just said.

"At . . . once?" she repeated almost beneath her breath. "But that is . . . impossible!"

"Not if you agree to what I suggest."

"And what is . . . that?"

"You can marry me!"

For a moment Andrina felt that she could not have heard him right.

Then as she put out her hand to hold on to the desk his eyes met hers, and she felt something strange and wonderful come alive within her.

They stood looking at each other and they were both very still.

It seemed to Andrina that she could no longer think, could hardly realise what was happening. It might have been a few seconds or several hours that passed before the Duke said:

"Will you give me an answer, Andrina? I am asking you to marry me."

"Why?"

He looked away from her and now he walked from the desk towards the mantelpiece to stand as he had done so often with his back to the fireplace.

"I need a wife," he said after a moment, and she thought that he had been feeling for words.

"Would . . . anyone do?"

Her voice was very low but he heard what she said.

"No—I want you!"

"But why?"

She hardly knew what she was saying, she felt a wild excitement sweeping through her body! The room was suddenly filled with sunlight and the angel voices she had heard in the Church were ringing in her ears.

"Must I give you an explanation?" the Duke enquired, and she had the feeling that he was deliberately forcing a harsh note into his voice. "I have asked you to marry me, Andrina. Surely that is enough?"

Very slowly Andrina walked from the desk towards him.

She stood looking at him and knew as she did so that what she saw in his eyes was very different from what he said with his lips.

She did not speak and after a moment he said almost impatiently:

"I am still waiting for your answer. Surely you can see that it is essential for you to be married now that your sisters are settled. You cannot live alone in the country, and therefore it is quite obvious you need a husband."

"It seems I have little . . . choice in the matter," Andrina murmured. "No-one . . . except Lord Crowhurst . . . has offered for me."

"As it happens," the Duke said, "there have been, I think, two Peers, a Baronet, several other eligible bachelors, and, damn his impertinence, a Frenchman!"

Andrina started and looked at him wide-eyed.

"You mean . . . you turned them away?"

"As your Guardian I did not consider them suitable!" the Duke said loftily.

"How dare you!" she exclaimed.

Yet she knew even as she spoke that it was her only too-familiar expression where he was concerned.

Even if all the men he had prevented from approaching her were now on their knees asking for her hand, she would find them as distasteful as she had Lord Crowhurst.

There was only one man she loved, one man who filled her life to the exclusion of all else, and he was asking her to marry him—but in a very strange fashion.

It was, however, understandable, now that she knew the secret which Mr. Robson had entrusted to her! But which for his sake she must never betray.

Perhaps one day the Duke would tell her himself what he had suffered.

"You had . . . no right to keep those . . . gentlemen from . . . speaking to me," she said a little weakly, knowing it was really of no importance.

"You were glad enough to be rid of Crowhurst," the Duke replied.

"That was . . . different," Andrina said. "He was . . . repulsive . . . as you well know."

"But a far better catch than all the others, and that, after all, was what you required in a husband. It is also unlikely from that point of view that you will do better than to marry me."

"You are quite . . . sure you wish to be . . . married?" Andrina queried.

"I cannot think of any other way that I can look after you," he replied. "You cannot stay on indefinitely in my house. It would give rise to too much gossip. Besides, I suppose there comes a time in every man's life when he should take a wife and settle down."

He paused, then said with that cynical twist of his lips that Andrina knew so well:

"I cannot find anyone better-looking, and you will certainly do justice to the Broxbourne jewellery!"

Andrina felt that he was deliberately building up his defences against her, armouring himself against any expression of his feelings, and yet she was not sure.

She loved him, she thought, so overwhelmingly that it was hard to think straight. Hard to be certain of anything except the tumultuous feelings within her breast.

She knew the Duke was awaiting her reply, confident, and sure of himself. Yet a super-sensitive perception told her that without revealing it he was tense.

"I am waiting for your answer, Andrina," the Duke said, "and of course impatiently!"

There was again that cynical note, but she was no longer afraid of it.

Clasping her hands together as if they gave her the courage she needed, she looked up at him and said in a very low voice, and yet every word was distinct:

"I thank Your Grace for your . . . offer of marriage. It is very flattering, but I must . . . decline the honour of being your . . . wife!"

She drew a deep breath. Then with her eyes on his she said:

"But because I . . . love you . . . because I want more than . . . anything else in the world to make you . . . happy . . . I will come to you and . . . belong to you as you wanted . . . me to do the first night we met."

The colour rose in Andrina's face and it was difficult to breath, but her eyes were still on the Duke's.

She saw the whole expression on his face change. Then he said, and his voice was surprisingly hoarse:

"Do you understand what you are saying?"

"I . . . understand," Andrina answered, "but because you would never . . . believe that I was not . . . marrying you for your . . . title rather than . . . for yourself . . . I want nothing from . . . you except your . . . love as a . . . man."

Her voice broke a little on the last word.

The Duke did not move. It seemed as if he was turned to stone. Then because she could not help herself, Andrina moved towards him and raised her face to his.

"Please . . . love me," she whispered. "I . . . love you with . . . all of me!"

Very slowly, it seemed to her, the Duke's arms went round her. Then he looked down into her upturned face with an expression of wonder in his eyes as if he could not believe what he saw.

Then slowly, very slowly, his lips found hers.

Just for a moment Andrina felt a sudden fear in case the magic had gone, but it was there! The forked-lightning swept through her body, a half pain—half a rapture that was beyond words, beyond expression!

It was what she had felt the first time he had kissed her, and yet it was more intense, more wonderful, and so incredibly glorious that she felt she was no longer herself but part of him.

The room whirled round her, the ceiling fell down on her head, the air was diffused with a golden, blinding light which seemed to come from the sun itself.

Then there was only the Duke's arms, his lips, and him in the whole world. . . .

*   *   *

Andrina sat in the big bed waiting.

As the maids had gone from the room after helping her undress, curtseying and murmuring: "Good-night, Your Grace," she wondered if she would ever get used to being a Duchess.

She could hardly realise that she was in fact married and that the Duke was her husband and she was his wife.

It was so typical of him, she thought, that he had everything planned even down to the Marriage-Licence which he had taken from a drawer in his desk.

"But I do not . . . intend to . . . marry you!" she had protested when he showed it to her.

"You will marry me!" he said fiercely. "Do you think I would risk losing you, allowing other men to approach you, not having you with me both day and night?"

"Then you had thought of . . . marrying me before . . . today?" she asked unnecessarily.

"Yes!"

"When did you first . . . want me as your . . . wife?"

He hesitated and she knew that he was finding it difficult to answer her.

"I had not finished kissing you in the Inn."

"Yet you would have been content never to see me again?"

There was a pause before he answered reluctantly:

"Actually, as soon as I reached London I sent a servant to the Coaching-Yard to make enquiries about you. He was naturally asking for a Miss Morgan. While he was doing so, Miss Maldon walked into my Library!"

"So the kiss was . . . wonderful for . . . you too!" Andrina said softly.

The Duke did not reply and she continued:

"You seemed to despise me, and everything I did made you angry."

Again there was silence until the Duke said gruffly:

"I was—jealous!"

"Why did you not . . . tell me so?"

"You were so insistent that you hated me. It did not surprise me. It was what I expected. At the same time, I wanted you and I did not intend to let any other man have you if I could possibly help it! So I sent away your hordes of admirers with what is vulgarly called 'a flea in the ear'!"

"I have a feeling that was cheating and not quite cricket!" Andrina said.

"I pay no attention to those sort of rules," the Duke replied loftily. "What I want, I take!"

Once again he was trying to make himself out to be a worse character than he really was, Andrina thought, and she made no further protests when he took her off to the Church where he had already arranged for a Parson to be waiting for them.

Only as they reached St. George's, having driven there almost in silence, Andrina said:

"You are quite . . . certain you wish to be married? I meant it in all sincerity when I said I would . . . stay with you without being your . . . wife."

"I know you did!" the Duke said.

He put out his hand and taking her chin in his fingers turned her face up to his.

"Do you suppose you could lie to me?" he asked. "I know every expression in your eyes, every inflection in your voice."

He paused and added almost violently:

"I cannot live without you—that is what you want me to say and now I have said it!"

Then as if he could not help himself he kissed her.

It was only a quick touch of their lips, because the horses were drawing to a standstill, but Andrina felt the fire which raged within him and the thrill of it made her quiver.

Theirs was a very different wedding from that of Cheryl and Sharon. There was no congregation, no choir, only the organ playing very softly.

The fragrance of the lilies scented the air and the shadows outside the circle of light cast by the candles on the altar seemed to be filled with invisible witnesses.

Andrina was sure that her mother was there, praying for her future happiness, and she thought that the Duke's mother was present too, wanting him to find the love he had lost when she died.

On her knees, holding his hand very tightly, Andrina prayed that somehow she could break through the barriers that surrounded him.

It was not going to be easy. There were years of pride, of cynicism and resentment, to be broken down, but somehow, with God's help, she knew she would manage it.

"Help me . . . please help me," she prayed. "Do not let me think of myself or my feelings, but only for him. Show me how to make him happy and keep me from making mistakes."

*   *   *

As they drove away from the Church the Duke kissed her fingers but he did not put his arms around her.

It was as if the solemn sanctitiy of the Service in which they had just taken part made it difficult for both of them for the moment to feel anything but detached from the world, and they drove back almost in silence.

There was a light meal waiting for them in a small room which had been hastily decorated with white flowers, and when it was finished the Duke and Andrina sat for a while talking.

Afterwards she could never remember what subjects they touched on; she only knew there were poignant silences when their hearts seemed to be speaking to each other and there was no need for words.

Then at length she had risen from the table, realising how late it was and that they had both had a long day.

The Duke walked with her to the bottom of the staircase in the Hall, and as she went upstairs alone she knew he was watching her until she disappeared.

She was not sleeping in the bed-room she had used since she had first arrived at Broxbourne House, but in a beautifully decorated room overlooking the garden, which, she was told, the Duchesses of Broxbourne had used for generations.

In it there was a large bed with blue silk curtains lined with muslin falling from a carved corona of gold angels.

There was a fairy-tale quality about it and the lace-edged pillows at Andrina's back were very soft. But she sat up, her back straight, her hair in the dim light from a single candle by the bed-side seeming full of mysterious shadows as it fell over her shoulders to her waist.

It seemed to her that she waited a very long time before she heard the door open, and when the Duke came into the room he seemed larger and more overpowering than usual.

Perhaps it was his velvet robe which reached to the ground, or perhaps because Andrina herself felt dwarfed by the great bed and the room which was larger than any she had slept in before.

As he came towards her she felt her heart beating a

little apprehensively, and there was a constriction in her throat which made it hard to swallow.

He stood looking at her, her eyes wide and worried in her small face and her hands clasped together in front of her on the white sheet.

"You are very beautiful!" he said at length.

"Not as beautiful as Cheryl or Sharon!"

"Can you really compare yourself to your lovely but nit-witted younger sister, or Sharon, who will in a few years make a polished, sophisticated Ambassadress?"

"You like my face . . . better . . . than theirs?"

"I find it impossible to look at any other woman when you are in the room!"

Andrina drew in her breath. He had never paid her a compliment before.

"But you have so much more than a beautiful face," he said almost as if he spoke to himself.

Then he sat down, facing her, on the side of the bed and said in a low voice:

"I am frightened, Andrina!"

Whatever else she had expected him to say it was not this, and as her eyes questioned him he said:

"You have said you love me. But if I frighten you or shock you, you may hate me again, and that I could not bear!"

Andrina drew in her breath.

Now she understood.

This was not the autocratic, overwhelming Duke who was speaking, but the little boy who had had everything he ever loved taken away from him, and he was afraid now of losing her.

This was the moment when she must pierce his defences and sweep them away.

For a moment she felt helpless and inadequate.

"I have forgotten how to be gentle, if I ever knew it!" the Duke went on. "I have grown used to being harsh and indifferent to anyone's feelings but my own."

His eyes were on her face as he said:

"But I care about yours! I want your love, I want it

desperately! Help me, Andrina, to be as you want me to be."

Suddenly Andrina no longer felt helpless, her heart told her what to do.

She smiled and it seemed to illuminate her whole face. Very simply she held out her arms.

"You will not frighten or shock me," she said softly. "I love you just as you are. I love you with all my heart ... my mind, and my ... soul! They are all yours, there is nothing else I can give ... you!"

The Duke made a strange sound and suddenly he bent towards her and as she slipped backwards against the pillows his face was hidden against her neck.

"Do you really—mean that?" he asked, and his voice was unsteady and strange, as if something had cracked within him.

Then as he held her against him so that it was hard to breathe Andrina felt something wet against her neck.

She knew in that moment that he needed her as Cheryl had done, or as one day her son would need her, and her arms went round him. She held him very close, her lips against his hair.

"I love you ... more than I can ever ... tell you!" she whispered, "and I know there are so ... many marvellous things for us to do ... together."

The Duke made no sound but he held her tighter as Andrina went on:

"But first there are so ... many things you have to ... teach me ... as you have said so often ... I am very ... foolish, and you are so ... wise."

She gave a little sigh.

"When we were being married I thought that if you were not a Duke ... if you had no money, I would have been able to prove more ... easily that I love you ... because you are you! But then I realised that you had told me already how ... unimportant such things ... are."

She could still feel the Duke's tears against her skin as she went on:

"I suddenly understood that when we are like this it does not matter if you are a Duke or a dustman! It is not important whether we are in a Palace or a garret! We are just two people together ... a man and a woman who must love each other ... otherwise everything we did would be horrible! But instead ... because I love you, it is like being in ... Heaven!"

The Duke raised his head.

Now in the faint light from the candle Andrina could see the tears on his cheeks but there was a touch of fire in his eyes.

"Can I make our love seem like Heaven to you, my darling?" he asked.

"To be ... close to ... you and when you kiss me is very wonderful," Andrina answered, "but I want to ... belong to you ... completely ... I want you to teach me about love ... the love that I have for you and I think you ... have for me."

She looked up at him and realised there was an expression on his face that made him look younger and happier than he had ever done before. It seemed to transform him. Then he said, his voice broken and unsteady:

"I love and worship you—my perfect little wife! You are the most beautiful person I have ever known and you are mine—all mine! I can never lose you, never let you go!"

"You will never lose me," Andrina whispered.

He was drawing her closer, his hands were wakening her body to strange sensations, his lips kindled a flame within her which echoed the fire in his eyes.

"Love me, my darling—love me! God knows how much I want your love!"

The words were repeated and repeated against her lips, her cheeks, her neck, her breasts.

"I love you ... I love ... you!"

She did not know if she spoke the words or they were in her mind.

Then they were both lost in an inexpressible ecstasy

which carried them away into a Heaven of their own!

Nothing the world could offer was of any consequence besides the rapture, the glory, and the wonder of love!

ABOUT THE AUTHOR

BARBARA CARTLAND, the celebrated romantic author, historian, playwright, lecturer, political speaker and television personality, has now written over 150 books. Miss Cartland has had a number of historical books published and several biographical ones, including that of her brother, Major Ronald Cartland, who was the first Member of Parliament to be killed in the War. This book had a Foreword by Sir Winston Churchill.

In private life, Barbara Cartland, who is a Dame of the Order of St. John of Jerusalem, has fought for better conditions and salaries for Midwives and Nurses. As President of the Royal College of Midwives (Hertfordshire Branch), she has been invested with the first Badge of Office ever given in Great Britain, which was subscribed to by the Midwives themselves. She has also championed the cause for old people and founded the first Romany Gypsy Camp in the world.

Barbara Cartland is deeply interested in Vitamin Therapy and is President of the British National Association for Health.

Barbara Cartland

The world's bestselling author of romantic fiction.
Her stories are always captivating tales of intrigue,
adventure and love.

Bantam Book Catalog

It lists over a thousand money-saving best-sellers originally priced from $3.75 to $15.00 —bestsellers that are yours now for as little as 50¢ to $2.95!

The catalog gives you a great opportunity to build your own private library at huge savings!

So don't delay any longer—send us your name and address and 25¢ (to help defray postage and handling costs).